LOVE ON SAFARI

When Marianne's fiancé, James, a famous fashion photographer, failed to turn up for their wedding, she was shocked and angry and made up her mind to seek revenge on his family. Knowing that James's seldom-mentioned older brother, Nicholas, was a veterinarian who ran safaris somewhere in South Africa, she decided to go and find him and make him fall in love with her! Marianne's manhunt turned out to be successful — but not quite in the way she had planned it!

Books by Beverley Winter
in the Linford Romance Library:

HOUSE ON THE HILL
A TIME TO LOVE
LOVE UNDERCOVER
MORTIMER HONOUR
THE HEART'S LONGING

BEVERLEY WINTER

LOVE ON SAFARI

Complete and Unabridged

LINFORD
Leicester

First published in Great Britain in 2003

First Linford Edition
published 2004

British Library CIP Data

Winter, Beverley
    Love on safari.—Large print ed.—
    Linford romance library
    1. Love stories
    2. Large type books
    I. Title
    823.9'14 [F]

    ISBN 1–84395–365–X

Published by
F. A. Thorpe (Publishing)
Anstey, Leicestershire

Set by Words & Graphics Ltd.
Anstey, Leicestershire
Printed and bound in Great Britain by
T. J. International Ltd., Padstow, Cornwall

This book is printed on acid-free paper

1

On the morning of her wedding, Marianne Chattan jumped out of bed, flung back the curtains and gave a small sigh of relief. The thick mist which had mantled the village for days was beginning to lift, wreathing the mountain behind the house in delicate garlands of gauze. The pale autumn sky would soon be filled with sunshine — a really happy omen if ever there was one!

'James would just hate it if it were to rain,' she murmured.

James Logan, her fiancé, liked everything to be perfect.

Marianne peered into the street below, where the sleepy Scottish village of Inchfarrel was for once very much awake, having discarded its usual lethargic pace for a buzz of excited activity. The caterers were offloading their van of equipment, old Mr Forbes was busy raking a few sodden brown leaves from the front lawn and several of the village children were already lining the street.

Marianne's glance turned to the splendid, bead-encrusted wedding gown hanging from a hook in the rafter of her attic bedroom, its ivory satin gleaming richly in the early-morning light. To be honest, it was a little too ornate for her taste, but James had been to a lot of trouble over it and she hadn't liked to make a fuss.

After all, as the bride of a famous fashion photographer, she was expected to look the part. James had commissioned the gown to be specially designed by one of his illustrious cronies from London, and what's more, it had cost the earth.

Setting a date for the wedding itself had been a logistical nightmare. After months of deliberation James had finally agreed that the ceremony would be sandwiched in between a lucrative shoot for a large mail-order catalogue, one or two of the more important fashion shows and his six-monthly dental appointment! James always kept his teeth in perfect condition!

'My career must come first,' he'd pointed out firmly. 'Besides, you know as well as I do that there are the instalments to meet on my new red Ferrari.'

Marianne sighed once more, aware that she wasn't quite as happy as she ought to be. Quickly she banished these vague misgivings, telling herself it was quite normal for a bride to have last-minute doubts.

Her mother, Mary Chattan, had planned the final hours before the ceremony with meticulous care, whilst her father, Dr Hamish Chattan, the local GP and busy up until the last moment, had gone to some considerable trouble to procure a locum so that he might be present to give his daughter away. It was to be the perfect, traditional family wedding.

Marianne gulped down the tea which Flora, their home help, had brought in earlier. Her parents, she reflected fondly, were such dears. They were pulling out all the stops for their only daughter, and she was determined to make them proud of her. She set the cup down in its saucer and went into the bathroom to run her bath.

In half an hour the hairdresser would be arriving to help her pile her long hair into a fashionable knot at the nape of her neck, complete with all those wispy strands which James so admired. The last time she'd worn her hair like that he'd kissed her and told her he couldn't wait to be married. It was to be hoped that once they had settled into married life James would pay her a little more attention.

Marianne poured a generous amount of bath salts into the water, reflecting that by this time James would be making his own preparations. He'd be cosily ensconced in the best suite at the Ben Wyvis Hotel in nearby

Strathpeffer, manfully rehearsing his wedding speech. Naturally he would want it to be perfect.

The ceremony was to take place in the small, sandstone church which stood no more than a hundred yards from the Chattan's front door. Her father was to escort her down the street at precisely five minutes to ten, and after the ceremony the guests would return to her parents' home for the wedding breakfast. This would be held in the big, striped marquee which had been erected on the lawn, complete with floral arrangements and crisp pink tablecloths. Already the caterers were hard at work setting out the glasses.

Marianne swirled the water with one perfectly manicured hand while her busy mind ran through the programme. By early afternoon everything would be over, and she and James could climb into James's new red Ferrari and begin their short, two-day honeymoon on the West Coast of Scotland. She would have preferred it to have been longer than two days but James had insisted that he couldn't spare the time. She very much feared that the real reason was that he would be bored, stuck in a tiny fishing village with nothing but birds to photograph — the wrong kind, of course.

At nine-fifty, Marianne, a punctual girl by nature, took one last look around her bedroom before descending the stairs, taking great care not to tread on her veil.

'You look beautiful, darling,' her mother told her, turning to peer into the hall mirror to ensure that the pink roses on her cream straw hat were perfectly aligned. 'I'll tell your father you're ready. Just give me a few moments to precede you to the church.'

Protocol, according to Mrs Chattan, had to be observed at all costs. Meanwhile, Dr Chattan, calm as ever, surveyed his daughter with pride as she took his arm.

'Good luck, lass,' he told her gruffly.

A group of villagers was gathered outside the house waiting to wish them well. They waved and cheered, for Dr Chattan was a popular man as well as a good physician. Smiling and unhurried, Marianne and her father began their short walk to the church.

Reverend MacIllvenny was waiting for them on the front steps. Marianne, preoccupied with keeping her veil under control, failed to notice the faint frown between his bushy eyebrows. Instead of preceding them into the church as had been arranged, the minister ushered them swiftly through the foyer and into the vestry on one side. Marianne, about to object, took one look at his face and fell silent. Reverend MacIllvenny cleared his throat.

'I'm afraid there has been a slight hitch,' he murmured unhappily.

Marianne gasped.

'Hitch? I don't understand.'

Everything had been planned with great care down to the last detail. How could there possibly be a hitch?

'Well, my dear, the bridegroom has not arrived.'

He cleared his throat and continued soothingly.

'No doubt he'll be here shortly, but until then it would be advisable for us to remain in the vestry, do you not agree?'

He surveyed Marianne's wedding gown doubtfully.

'Would you like to sit down?'

Marianne swallowed her disappointment.

'No, thank you, I'll stand. James is bound to arrive at any moment. He's often late for things. It's his artistic temperament, you see.'

She peered up at her father's calm face. It revealed nothing of his thoughts, but his daughter knew him better than that. She had detected a decided glint of anger in his dark eyes.

She murmured unhappily, 'I'm sorry, Father.'

'Good heavens, lass, it's not your fault,' Dr Chattan growled, and turned to the minister, an old family friend, and confided, 'I have to confess that I take a dim view of this, John.'

The good doctor was soon to take an even dimmer view.

Forty minutes later, his prospective son-in-law had still not arrived, the congregation was growing restive and his dear wife was valiantly holding back the tears. As for Marianne, her white, set face told its own story. Tight-lipped, the doctor strode to the desk.

'May I use the telephone, John?'

'Go ahead, Hamish,' the minister agreed crisply.

In all his years of conducting weddings, he'd never once had a late bridegroom to contend with. It was usually the bride who indulged in such practices! He watched as Dr Chattan dialled the number of the reception at Ben Wyvis Hotel.

'I wish to speak to Mr James Logan, please.'

He listened intently to the voice on the other end, thanked the clerk with icy politeness and replaced the receiver with a sharp click.

'They say there is no such person staying at the hotel.'

Marianne went even paler.

'But that's impossible! Mother confirmed the booking only yesterday morning.'

Her father gave her a pitying look.

'So she did, my dear. The suite was indeed reserved but the unsavoury fact remains that your fiancé has not bothered to show up.'

Marianne felt a terrible, sick anxiety in the pit of her stomach. The ghastly suspicion which had been forming for the last ten minutes looked as though it had just been confirmed. She was not to be married today after all.

'He . . . he may have had an accident somewhere on the way up from London,' she stammered a little wildly. 'He may be lying in a hospital bed somewhere!'

'I doubt it,' Dr Chattan drawled.

He'd had no great opinion of James Logan from the time they'd met and considered him to be a selfish, ambitious young man who gave no thought to the comfort or feelings of others.

'Marianne, I suggest that you telephone James's London apartment.'

'Yes, yes, of course.'

Trying to master a sense of panic, Marianne lifted the receiver with a shaking hand and dialled the number she knew off by heart. It rang for quite some time before she heard James's voice in a recorded announcement informing her that he was out of the country and therefore not available to take her call. Marianne stared at her father in shocked miscry.

'I'll phone his artist friend, Grant Colby,' she cried, trying to mask her anguish and quite failing to do so. 'He lives in the flat next door. I'm certain he will know where James is.'

Marianne lifted the receiver again, feeling as though she was operating on auto-pilot. This could not possibly be happening to her! The impatient young man who answered the call listened for a moment and then told her coldly, 'I wish you'd stop pestering James,

Marianne. He has his own life to live, you know.'

Marianne could hardly believe her ears.

'Pestering him? I have a perfect right to pester him, as you put it! Do you realise that today is the day of our wedding? James is supposed to be at the church in Inchfarrel. In fact, he should have been here at least an hour ago. I must know where he is. Where is he?'

'How should I know?'

There was a faint sneer behind the words.

'He's most probably out on an important photographic assignment. You of all people should know that he is much in demand.'

Marianne took a deep breath in order to calm herself.

'I do know that,' she gritted through her perfect white teeth, 'but that does not alter the fact that we are to be married today. I happen to know that he took great pains to clear his diary for the occasion.'

Grant sniggered.

'Did he, now?'

Something in his attitude alerted Marianne.

'You know exactly where he is, don't you?' she said slowly.

'What if I do?'

Anger writhed deep within her.

'I want you to tell me where he is, Grant. The least my fiancé could do is explain himself!'

Grant gave a snort.

'The great James Logan need not explain himself to anyone, least of all some hysterical female on the end of a telephone. But for the record, something important came up during the week. He is otherwise occupied.'

'Doing what?'

Grant Colby gave a derisive laugh.

'If you must know, he took a sudden assignment to photograph the current Miss England for a travel magazine.'

Marianne felt the breath leave her chest.

'I see. May I ask where?'

'Oh, they flew off to a game park somewhere,' Grant admitted casually. 'South Africa, I think it was.'

'South Africa!'

'I believe so. James met her last month at a party in London, and when her agent subsequently telephoned with the offer, he felt it was too good an opportunity to miss. Surely you can see that.'

With clear hindsight Marianne certainly could. James had always put his own interests first. The unwelcome truth dawned on her that their relationship had not been a healthy one. Throughout their time together she'd been the one to make all the adjustments in the mistaken belief that it had been her job to keep him happy at all costs. James was a demanding young man and she had slipped into the rôle of pleaser. What a fool she'd been! Mature relationships demanded equality, with each partner putting the other's interests first.

'No, I can't see it,' she retorted

coldly. 'James's priorities are all wrong.'

'You'll turn into a nagging, old maid, Marianne. No man in his right mind will have you after this. I daresay James is having a fabulous time. He intends contacting some of his long-lost relatives out there, says they'll give him a free holiday, and show him a bit of the country at the same time. I told him to go for it.'

Marianne gave an unladylike snort. How like James to turn everything to his own advantage!

'So you do understand, Marianne, that James Logan will not be tying any knot today, with you or anyone else. It's your own fault, anyway,' he observed cruelly. 'You're such an old-fashioned, country frump, with your goody-two-shoes airs. It's no wonder James was so taken with Miss England.'

Marianne did not wait to hear any more. She slammed down the telephone. Dr Chattan and the minister were viewing her in consternation.

'There'll be no wedding today,' she

told them tightly, her face a blank mask. 'I apologise for the inconvenience.'

Marianne turned large, anguished eyes on her father, unable to make any sense out of what was happening and too numbed to even try. The world had begun to spin about her and her stomach was churning in a most unpleasant manner. All hope was gone. The day she'd anticipated for so long had turned into a total nightmare. Her life would never be the same again, and what's more, she wanted to be sick.

Dr Chattan exchanged a few grim words with the minister, placed a comforting arm about his daughter's shoulders and murmured soothingly in her ear. Marianne didn't hear a word.

The unpleasant task of informing everyone fell to Reverend MacIllvenny, whose announcement in the church was greeted with murmurs of shocked disbelief. Mrs Chattan gave a small cry and slumped in her pew while the guests filed out of he church in a dejected little group.

Accustomed to emergencies of every description, Dr Chattan immediately took charge. He escorted his distraught wife and daughter back to the privacy of their home where he dismissed the bewildered caterers, arranged to phone their manager on Monday and shooed them all from the house. Feeling utterly humiliated, Mrs Chattan removed her hat and shepherded her unhappy daughter into the living-room where Marianne, alone with her parents, finally burst into tears.

Dr Chattan placed a mug of brandy-laced tea into his daughter's hands.

'Drink up, there's a good lass,' he encouraged.

'I'll never,' Marianne sobbed, 'forgive James for this, never. He's an utter toad!'

'All that food!' Mrs Chattan wailed.

Dr Chattan patted his wife's hand.

'I am sure the residential home in Strathpeffer will be delighted to receive it, my dear. Imagine how the old folk would enjoy such a treat.'

Mrs Chattan sniffed.

'Even so. I shall never be able to see a quiche or carrot cake again without remembering.'

She blew her nose and added with unaccustomed venom, 'That young man ought to be horse-whipped!'

A sentiment with which her husband privately agreed. He continued to hold his peace, however, while his wife was allowed the luxury of a few sharp words. Dr Chattan considered the situation regrettable but not dire, for he had seen too much of life not to be able to hold things in perspective. They must look on the positive side. Marianne had been saved from what would undoubtedly have been an unfortunate marriage.

'Such an insult!' Mrs Chattan muttered wrathfully.

The insult, however, was far from complete.

She was to become even more

incensed when her daughter received a registered letter in the post a week or so later. It arrived as they were having breakfast, and gave her quite the worst attack of indigestion she'd ever had.

The letter was from James Logan's London solicitor who informed Miss Marianne Chattan that he had been instructed to warn her that if she tried to make contact with Mr Logan by post, telephone or in person, she would be served with a county court injunction. Marianne went white with indignation.

'As if I'm a . . . a stalker, or something! All I did was telephone him on the day of the wedding in order to get some answers,' she blazed, 'and now I'm being threatened with legal action!'

'Take no notice,' her father advised calmly. 'That is the defensive action of a foolish young man who knows he's in the wrong. Cut your losses, Marianne, and consider yourself well rid.'

Marianne bit viciously into her toast. 'Too right, I am! It is painfully obvious that he didn't love me at all, Father. I can see it all clearly now. I attracted him because I'm a different type of girl from the ones he usually dates, and I represented a challenge. I'm old-fashioned, you see. I respect marriage.'

She stirred a spoonful of sugar into her coffee and tasted the liquid without realising just how hot it was. With a small wince of pain, she put the cup down.

'We would never have been compatible in the end. The fact that I was prepared to entrust my entire future to him is a scary thought.'

Her pretty mouth tightened into a thin line.

'I was a fool not to have seen the kind of man he is. They say love is blind. Well, I was not only blind, I was deaf and dumb as well!'

Marianne helped herself to another slice of toast and lavished on the butter. Who cared if she got fat now?

'In the end it simply boils down to

the one thing, Father. James is utterly selfish. He betrayed my trust, which means that he is either terribly weak or frighteningly cruel.'

'Probably both,' Mrs Chattan retorted as she rose to clear the table. 'I can't understand it, Marianne. You're a decent, hard-working girl, with friends and family who respect you. Why did he do it?'

With a sigh her husband folded up his newspaper and laid it to one side.

'James is the type of self-serving young man who hasn't the courage or strength of character to do what is right.'

He gave his daughter an intent glance.

'The important thing, Marianne, is not to allow one unfortunate experience to colour the rest of your life.'

Too late, Marianne thought bitterly. How could she just shake it off? She would never, ever trust a man again!

'You will find happiness one day,' her father added, just as though he'd read her thoughts. 'There are plenty of solid, trustworthy men out there, my dear.

21

Let us pray that you find one.'

Marianne snorted.

'I have no intention whatsoever of finding another man, Father, solid or otherwise. Men are more trouble than they are worth!'

The following week, Marianne returned to the clinic where she worked as a veterinary nurse and handed in her resignation. She'd had plenty of time to consider the matter during the preceding days, having taken numerous long walks up the glen with the family dogs.

These quiet days had soothed her turmoil to some extent, but she was left with a fierce, seething restlessness which simply would not go away.

Her boss, Mr Longmore, looked up from his desk.

'Ah, Marianne.'

His gaze was sympathetic, for his wife had informed him privately about Marianne's recent misfortunes.

'I can quite understand your need for a change of scene, my dear, but are you sure you wish to take such a drastic step? If you should change your mind . . . '

Stubbornly Marianne shook her head.

'I'll not change my mind, sir.'

'A pity. We'll be sorry to lose you. You've done sterling work here. May I ask what your future plans are?'

Marianne considered for a moment. She had been mulling over the possibility for days, and the decision was as good as made. One way or another she intended to get even with James Logan, and if for some reason that was not possible, she'd hit on another member of his rotten family. The Logans needn't think they could get away with this!

She wasn't normally a vengeful person, but then, she'd never been stood up at the altar before, had she? What's more, she was perfectly entitled to revenge. Nobody, but nobody, was to be allowed to insult her family in this way and get away with it!

Until now, Marianne had always

considered herself to be a polite, congenial little ray of sunshine; a gentle, co-operative girl with uncomplicated tastes, like enjoying a walk in the country, or caring for dumb animals, or making the rowan jelly to go with the venison. She'd wanted a peaceful life, which is doubtless why she'd so frequently allowed James to have his own way, even the matter of choosing a wedding gown. What a wimp she'd been!

With sobering insight, Marianne realised that the experience of James's rejection had changed her profoundly. From now on men beware! All that remained now was for her to sharpen her claws in readiness for the fight. The Chattans were a proud lot. They would fight tooth and nail to avenge an insult, as the Logan family would discover to their cost!

Deliberately she ticked them off in her mind. There was the obnoxious James, his rather uppity sister, Harriet, and his seldom-mentioned, much older brother, Nicholas, the son of his father's first wife. She couldn't quite remember where he lived, but she would find out.

She found out he was a veterinarian of note who ran some sort of reserve for wild animals in South Africa, where they ran safaris for overseas guests. He sounded like the perfect victim!

Unaware of her boss's growing impatience, Marianne took a further moment to savour her plans. She'd go to South Africa, find the man and make him fall in love with her!

A small, small, secret smile curved her lips.

She'd sweetly agree to the wretched man's proposal of marriage when it came and then walk out on the eve of their so-called wedding. What could be easier? After that she'd return to Scotland to her job as a veterinary nurse and get on with her life, hopefully without this unspeakable feeling of restlessness. Perhaps then she'd find a little peace.

Mr Longmore, waiting impatiently for her answer, glanced at his watch. Clients were becoming restless in the waiting-room. He coughed.

'Marianne?'

Marianne beamed at him, her mind quite made up.

'I'm going to Africa,' she stated.

'Good heavens, girl, why there?'

Marianne hesitated just briefly and then spoke the perfect truth.

'I'm interested in wild animals, sir. I've always wanted to view them in their natural habitat, and what better way to do so? I shall go on a safari.'

Mr Longmore nodded absently, his mind already on the morning ahead.

'Enjoy yourself then, my dear, and remember, you will always be welcome back here. You may leave at the end of the week.'

Marianne thanked him gravely, hiding a grin. What would the dear man say if he knew the truth?

She could hardly have announced, 'I'm on a mission to find, view and ensnare a certain, detestable wild animal of the male human variety. And when I'm finished with said animal, he'll wish he'd never heard the name of Chattan!'

2

The dust from the thirsty African bushland had been whipped into great golden clouds by an early summer wind and the air was thick with heat and silence.

The animals were growing restless in anticipation, for soon the smell of rain falling heavily on the parched earth would fill their nostrils and they would be forced to seek shelter in the dense undergrowth.

Dr Nicholas Logan, known among his friends and colleagues as Nico, lifted his binoculars and watched a lioness slink with lazy grace through the long, tawny grass. For once the animal was completely uninterested in the herd of antelope grazing nearby, for she had made her kill the precious evening and was well satisfied.

A small smile of satisfaction curved

Nico's firm mouth. The animal appeared to have recovered well from the treatment he'd performed two weeks previously, when he'd found her badly mauled from an encounter with a warthog. The warthog, an animal whose tusks are known to be lethal, had disappeared into the bush, apparently none the worse for the experience.

Nico put his open-top Jeep into gear and moved forward over the rough, grassy terrain. His eyes were narrowed against the glare of the sun as he scanned the endless landscape stretching to the distant, scrub-covered hills. A renowned conservationist and wild-life veterinarian, he was responsible for the vast Matonga Reserve to the north of South Africa, a duty he embraced with the utmost dedication.

Tall and tanned, with short, wavy dark hair and intelligent, slate-grey eyes, he kept himself in peak physical condition. The type of life he had led necessitated long hours in the harsh, sun-drenched African bush, supervising scientific breeding programmes, conserving the environment and working to prevent the extinction of certain endangered animal species in his care — not to mention the management of any foreign guests to the reserve.

The latter was a task he by no means relished. Tourists, Nico considered, were a necessary evil, especially the female of the species! He wasn't a conceited man but he knew that he was attractive to the opposite sex. It didn't help that he was no longer married, either, not that the presence of a wedding ring would deter some of the types who appeared on the reserve from time to time, he reflected ruefully. There was always some beauty in a skimpy pair of shorts casting blatant eyes in his direction, begging to accompany him and then showing not the slightest interest in any of the animals. The women were nothing but a darned nuisance!

He had a considerable staff of wardens under him, all housed in neat, thatched rondavels near the visitors' hutted camp. These huts were very basic, thatched structures with logged walls, used overnight by those who wished to experience an African safari. For safety purposes the whole area, including his own large bungalow, was enclosed by tall, electric fences.

Guests would be driven outside the enclosure in open-sided vehicles to the water holes and other viewing areas in order to watch the various species of game. In the evenings they would return, hot and tired, to relax under the stars and dine around camp fires if they so wished, where they would be entertained by the guitar-wielding wardens with their ethnic songs and exciting tales of the African bush.

Nico tossed his binoculars on to the seat beside him as the promised rain began its descent, falling suddenly and heavily upon the wide landscape. Lightning forked across the sky and thunder crashed deafeningly about his ears as the deluge hit his windscreen.

Imperturbably, Nico reached to close the top of the Jeep before turning in the direction of his home.

'It's raining hippos and rhinos today,' Nico murmured in satisfaction, turning the windscreen wipers up a notch in order to increase visibility.

The winter drought was breaking properly at last. Skilfully he negotiated the ruts in the dirt road, avoiding the larger ones. He allowed his thoughts to dwell briefly on the uneventful evening which lay ahead, a prospect which gave him no pleasure.

Jeremiah, his African cook, would doubtless have concocted one of his indifferent stews. This would most certainly be followed by an even more boring desert. Blancmange, perhaps? Nico gave a shudder. Perhaps tonight's offering would be bread pudding!

'What you need, Logan,' he told himself mockingly, 'is a wife.'

Strangely enough, the thought was not as abhorrent as it had been some months previously. He must be going soft! A wife — someone who would understand his job, run his home on oiled wheels and produce something at least faintly edible for the two of them on a fairly regular basis. Was that too much to ask?

Nico rounded a bend and gave a small grin. A wife would be a definite step in the right direction if he wished to repel the man-hunters. She wouldn't necessarily even have to be beautiful, not that he didn't appreciate nice-looking women, but he'd long since learned to distrust pretty women. They always had a secret agenda.

Men, on the other hand, were always upfront.

Nico changed gear as he negotiated the hill near his office complex, determined to avoid the main entrance to the enclosure where a uniformed guard stood sentry. Instead, he nosed the vehicle down a muddy track alongside the fence. There was a gate at the end of it, which led to his own private quarters.

After dinner, he reflected idly, there would be paperwork to see to, guns to clean and the latest veterinary journal to read. Then he would watch a little television, have a beer and take himself off to his lonely bed. Not that he really minded living alone. It was a lot less hassle than having to deal with a bored woman! In his experience, women grew bored easily.

An elderly, very wet elephant trundled across the path before him.

'Good afternoon, Nando,' Nico greeted him pleasantly. 'How's the digestion this week?'

Ignoring Nico's concern, the animal paused to peer short-sightedly at the truck. Nico slowed down and continued mockingly.

'What you need is a mate, my friend, someone to take your mind off your problems by giving you fresh ones.'

He smiled mirthlessly.

'Women, you see, have no depth. They nurture a constant wish to be entertained: Trouble is, you don't find theatres, beauty parlours and boutiques in the bush, do you?'

Having heard enough, the old bull stared haughtily down his trunk and plunged into the sodden undergrowth. Nico watched the animal's departing rump and delivered his parting shot.

'What's more, women are pathologically incapable of fidelity. I, Nicholas Logan, have the scars to prove it.'

Hadn't Carina come to hate bush life? She'd left him, to resume her medical career in Johannesburg and it had taken him years to recover, especially since she'd seen fit to abandon their sickly, eight-month-old daughter in the process. Nico shook his head and frowned. It was all in the past, and he had decided that he would never take another wife. So why was he indulging in pathetic pipe dreams?

Bleakly Nico revved the engine and made for home. At the thought of his small offspring, his heart twisted. Jenna's headmistress had telephoned to inform him that the child was not settling at her new school. She was persistently homesick, professing to hate the boarding establishment and crying in her bed at night.

He'd done his best to raise the child to be independent, but the truth was, she still lacked confidence. He must face the unpalatable truth. She needed a mother. He lifted a hand from the steering-wheel and raked it helplessly through his thick, dark hair.

His daughter had declared that she wished to continue living at home, but transporting her to school and back each day was just not feasible. It was a round drive of forty minutes each time, and he had a reserve to run. Now, if he had a wife . . .

Nico's eyes widened, his interest caught by a sudden movement in the grass near the fence. Beyond the fence, outside the reserve, wound the tarred road leading to Sunrise Lodge, a rather upmarket guest house run by that very merry widow indeed, Davina Delahunt. Davina had been pursuing him for months and had made it clear that she intended to become the second Mrs Logan. Nico had no intention of obliging her, but the woman didn't know the meaning of the word 'no'. Besides, Jenna didn't like her.

Nico slowed the vehicle to a halt, intent on finding out which animal it was that had gained his attention. He was accustomed to the pattern of a wild animal's movements and prided himself on being able to identify almost any animal at almost any distance. He narrowed his gaze, straining to see through the pelting rain. Suddenly he stiffened.

That was no animal — it was a human being. There'd been a flash of red clothing as the man had dashed into the undergrowth. Nico felt his blood begin to boil. His hands clenched the steering-wheel and his jaw hardened. If anything infuriated him out of his mind, it was this!

There had been a spate of senseless killings of late, the ruthless and wanton destruction of Matonga's elephant population by greedy poachers intent on selling the ivory — and this was undoubtedly one of them, trying to find shelter in the storm. Swiftly he reached for the shotgun he always kept on the seat beside him, and leaving the door open and the engine running, he flung himself into the sodden foliage in hot pursuit.

He didn't have far to run. The offender was crouched under a small thorn bush, trying to avoid the worst of the rain. He wore a navy knitted cap pulled low over his eyes, a red padded rain jacket and tight blue jeans. Nico flung down his gun and tackled the man with all speed, hauling him to his feet and slamming his slight body against a nearby tree.

'What the blazes do you think you're doing?' he demanded coldly.

A blank, terrified look appeared on the poacher's face. He uttered a soundless croak, apparently having lost the power of speech. Nico repeated himself grimly.

'Answer me, man! What are you doing here?'

Apart from his illegal activities, the man was in inherent danger from the wildlife itself. Didn't he know he could be killed and eaten? Nico's hands closed tightly over the man's wet shoulders. He gave them a rough shake.

'I said, what are you doing in this reserve?'

The poacher continued to stare like a mesmerised rabbit, his rather striking violet eyes enormous in his white face. The soft, well-shaped lips quivered as a few soundless words still hovered upon them, seemingly unable to escape.

'Got a mouthful of your own heart, have you?' Nico jeered, noting with satisfaction the way a frantic pulse was beating at the man's throat.

He was shaking like a wet dog, too. Serve him right! The poacher seemed awfully young; not more than about seventeen, small for a man, too. He'd have to stand up to look a snake in the eye, Nico thought. Perhaps if he really put the fear of God into the young man, there would be a chance he'd mend his ways before he got into serious trouble.

He growled, 'I am sure you must know that what you are doing is illegal?' and proceeded with relish to point out the penalties for the illegal and wanton destruction of valuable animals in a national park.

The rain was saturating Nico's shoulders and trickling down the collar of his bush jacket. He'd had a long day, he was tired and hungry, and his patience was wearing thin.

'Answer me, dammit, or I'll turn you into worm medicine,' he grated, giving the boy another rough shake.

In reply, the young man twisted sharply out of his grasp and fled, taking off into the undergrowth like some terrified quarry. Naturally Nico took off after him. He flung his large body at the boy's legs in one of the effective flying tackles he'd learned during his rugby days. It had the desired result. Both men fell heavily to the ground and rolled about in combat, grunting and panting in the slimy grass.

Nico, being by far the stronger, quickly straddled the boy's body. He yanked his arms behind his back, ignoring the quick cry of pain and the mouthful of mud the poacher appeared to have gathered in the process.

'Weapon?' he clipped, feeling roughly for a concealed knife or gun.

With a startled oath, his hands suddenly stilled. There was a trim, little waist, which flared into a shapely pair of hips, and there was a snug-fitting pair of jeans covering a delightful pair of legs, which appeared to know no end.

'Good grief, man!' Nico thundered. 'You're a woman!'

He jumped up in embarrassment and assisted the hapless female to her feet where he stood gazing down at her, at a complete loss for words. Of all the confounded things to happen!

'Of course I'm a woman, you fool!'

the poacher yelled, having found her voice at last. 'And you can remove your grubby, insulting paws this instant, or I'll . . . I'll . . . '

Nico folded his arms across his great chest and surveyed the woman with considerable interest from a considerable height.

'Or you'll what?'

The woman gave an unladylike cough and spat out a mouthful of mud.

'Or I'll turn you into . . . parasite medication, I think it was?' She coughed again. 'This mud tastes foul.'

Nico's lips twitched.

'It probably does,' he agreed pleasantly. 'These are our first proper rains of the season and by my reckoning it should taste like the sole of a two-year-old boot with the manure still on.'

The woman stared back, her chalky face a decided tinge of green. Concerned, Nico reached into his breast pocket for a handkerchief.

'Allow me,' he muttered, feeling foolish.

How could he have been so insensitive? The girl was about to be ill all over those impressive jeans of hers. Furiously she grabbed the cloth from his hand and proceeded to scrub the mud from her face. When she'd finished she thrust it back at him and fixed him with an indignant glare.

'Tell me something, mister. Are you in the habit of attacking every woman you meet, or is it just during the first rains of the season that you experience such an urge?'

Nico went a dull red.

'I wasn't attacking you. Well, in a manner of speaking . . . '

He broke off, gazing at her in genuine concern.

'Truth is, ma'am, I thought you were a poacher. You have my profound apologies.'

'A poacher?'

The woman looked incredulous.

'And you thought you'd caught me in the act, is that it? You're worse than a demented lioness with a starving family!'

She threw her hands into the air, her eyes sparkling with anger.

'Let me enlighten you, then, Mister Tarzan. I do not support animal cruelty in any way, shape or form. Get it? I'm a veterinary nurse, for pity's sake. It's my job to save animals, not destroy them!'

Nico's eyes gleamed beneath their lids.

'Is that a fact? Well, if you want to live another day to keep on saving 'em, I suggest you get your pretty little butt out of here pronto because you are at a distinct risk of being eaten by the morning.'

He took her by the arm and marched her firmly back to the truck.

'Get in, lady.'

The woman hesitated, peering up into his face.

'What do you mean, eaten?' she gulped.

'This is big cat territory, ma'am.'

The violet eyes widened.

'You mean, lions and such?'

'The same, plus a few cheetahs, leopards, lynxes and sundry other felines.'

He glanced down at her immaculately manicured hands.

'You may pride yourself on having a good set of claws, lady, but you're out of your league, take it from me. Now, will you please get in?'

The woman wasted no further time in hopping into the vehicle.

'I take it you've strayed here from Sunrise Lodge in the next valley?' Nico asked, concealing his irritation. 'The warden at the main entrance had no right to let you in here on foot.'

He would need to have a firm word with whoever was on duty. The guards knew perfectly well that only vehicles were permitted access to the reserve.

He continued resignedly, 'Allow me to give you a lift back.'

To his surprise, the woman shook her head.

'I'm not staying at Sunrise Lodge.'

Nico closed the passenger door and went around to the driver's seat. The crazy female appeared to be utterly clueless when it came to personal safety in a game reserve. He climbed into the driver's seat and shot her an exasperated glance.

'You're staying at our hutted camp then? I'll drive you back.'

He added severely, 'I would advise you not to stray outside the camp enclosure again, lady. It's too dangerous.'

Trust a woman to break the rules!

Controlling his mounting frustration, Nico let out the clutch. He was already late for the evening meal and Jeremiah would be waiting to go off duty. Conscious that his head was beginning to ache, he tried to concentrate on his driving. The light had gone, the rain was coming down even harder, and visibility was almost nil. Come to think of it, he hadn't been feeling his usual self all week.

'I'm not staying at the hutted camp,'

the woman said clearly.

Nico's eyebrows shot up.

'Where, then?'

She surely wasn't expecting him to taxi her all the way back to civilisation?

'I'm staying in that big, thatched bungalow over there, the one with those big electric gates, but they won't open. I did try ringing the bell,' she explained in an aggrieved tone.

Nico's jaw dropped.

'I beg your pardon?'

'The bell,' she repeated. 'I pushed the intercom button, but no-one answered. I decided to leave my hired car under those trees over there and explore around a bit. Then it started to rain and I had to dash for shelter. That's when you attacked me.'

Nico brought the truck to a screeching halt. Despite its enormous tyres it slewed violently in the mud.

'Let's get this straight. You say you're staying here in that thatched bungalow?'

'That's what I said, yes.'

Nico's eyes narrowed.

'With whom?' he asked, not believing what he was hearing.

'Um, with a Dr Nicholas Logan. I don't actually know the man.'

'No,' Nico agreed through clenched teeth. 'You certainly don't.'

'I'm told he's awful,' the woman confided. 'Very clever academically, but hasn't a clue about females unless they belong to the animal kingdom.'

She watched him carefully from beneath her lashes.

'In fact, I was distinctly told that he dislikes them, women, I mean.'

There was a moment's stunned silence.

'Dislikes them?' Nico repeated in a choked voice.

He was a normal male, for heaven's sake. It wasn't that he had an aversion to women, he simply treated them with a cynical, amused tolerance. It was safer that way.

He demanded silkily, 'May I ask who told you all this?'

'Oh, yes. It was a relative of his. James Logan, a man I once knew.'

Nico uttered something short and sharp under his breath. James the Jerk was at it again! He might have known that a man who could steal another man's wife wasn't above spreading rumour and innuendo, not that he, Nicholas Logan, gave a fig for his so-called reputation, or what the likes of this woman thought! Besides, any friend of James's was no friend of his, which made it even more imperative that he remain impervious to the appealing expression in those violet eyes.

'Personally,' the woman declared airily, 'I believe that all Dr Logan needs is a good woman, one who will change his outlook for him.'

And I intend to be that woman, she thought, at least, until just before the wedding ceremony!

Nico's mouth thinned.

'Is that so? I don't know who you are, lady, or what you want, but you are not staying in my home, and that's final.'

The lovely violet eyes widened.

'Your home? You are Nicholas Logan?'

She appeared to digest the information without batting an eyelid.

'Whoever would have thought it?'

'Who the dickens are you?' Nico demanded.

Thrusting out a slender hand tipped with pearly pink, she gave him the benefit of her brilliant smile. Nico blinked.

'My name is Marianne Chattan, and I am very pleased to meet you, Doctor Logan.'

Nico would have loved to ignore the hand, but good manners dictated otherwise. He covered it with his large one and promptly let it go. The current which passed between them had been hot enough to melt marshmallows. Marianne's smile even lit her extraordinary eyes, turning them into brilliant, coloured glass.

Nico controlled his breathing and stared back coolly. He refused to be deceived by the smile or the eyes, incredible as they both were. She offended him, pure and simple. This woman was on the make, and he was a man who preferred to do the running. He shook his head in order to clear it. The headache was becoming worse, which was unfortunate, because he needed an objective brain to decide what to do.

'What exactly do you want?' he snapped.

'Actually,' she said and allowed her gaze to rove his face, 'I'm looking for a job. James explained that you were running the Matonga Reserve and are an extremely busy man. We thought you might need a little help. I hoped that you would be able to employ me as a veterinary nurse, or some sort of secretary, or even as a cleaner, because I'm willing to do anything. I'd be very grateful.'

Nico looked incredulous.

'And on this very flimsy hope you've come all the way from wherever it is,

Scotland, by the sound of things, in order to insinuate yourself into my household? Lady, you have a colossal cheek!'

A fiery red crept into Marianne's cheeks, partly because she knew full well it was true. She was being awfully rude, but she had a purpose to fulfil and she would not be deflected from it. Normally she was both good mannered and good natured. She hardly recognised herself these days!

'You needn't make it sound as though I'm asking for charity, Doctor Logan,' she snapped. 'I am accustomed to hard work and I fully intend to deliver it!'

Despite her feisty words, her heart sank at his thunderous expression. Then a sudden flash of inspiration came to her rescue.

'You received the letter, didn't you?'

'What letter?'

'James Logan's letter,' Marianne improvised shamelessly, quelling her conscience.

She wasn't given to telling lies, either. In fact she detested deception, but she had no option, had she? She intended to extract revenge, and the means would simply have to justify the end! She took a deep breath.

'James,' she explained, 'wrote you a few weeks ago to say I would be arriving, and as you did not reply, we took it that you were in agreement. I've given up my job in Scotland, and everything.'

Nico close his eyes in an effort to ease the indescribable pain beneath his eyelids. His joints were beginning to ache, too.

'I received no such letter,' he said wearily.

Marianne thought quickly, looking for another tack.

'James said . . . well . . . that you must be lonely living all by yourself in the wilds, and that you might appreciate a little female companionship.'

A spasm crossed Nico's face, whether

of anger or amusement she couldn't tell.

'So the two of you decided to help poor old Nico along, did you? Tell me, Ms Chattan,' he demanded outrageously, 'are you any good?'

The blush, which had died down in Marianne's cheeks, rekindled vividly.

'I don't . . . I'm not . . . that wasn't . . . isn't quite what he . . . we meant,' she stammered.

Nico smiled nastily.

'Then what exactly did you mean? What is it exactly that you want from me? I don't buy the obviously fabricated request for a job.'

Marianne took a deep breath.

'It's true, you know. I want you to employ me. When I told James I was desperately keen to work with wild animals, he offered your assistance. He said you'd be delighted to help me.'

'Enough!' Nico rasped.

The mere mention of James's name was enough to send his blood pressure right into next week. As he remembered, the man had no compunction whatsoever about using people, and now the odious son of his selfish stepmother was up to something again, something which appeared to involve him, with this crazy woman, here, in cahoots! He would dearly love to know what they were up to but at this moment he felt too ill to care.

'I am prepared to put you up for one night only, Miss Chattan. Tomorrow I shall drive you to Sunrise Lodge where you will have to make other arrangements. What you do after that is no concern of mine.'

Nico drew up outside the gates of his home and activated the automatic mechanism, which opened them.

He said stonily, 'You may bring your car inside for the night.'

After parking his vehicle in the garage, with ill-concealed impatience he watched while she drove her hired green car into the space alongside it. As she climbed out and gave a small stretch, Nico's eyes raked her body in a cool, assessing stare.

'How old are you, anyway?'

Nico's breath caught. That hair was incredible, rippling like a banner in the breeze.

'Almost old enough to be your father,' he retorted, 'so don't get any ideas.'

Marianne gasped.

'You needn't be so rude! For your information, I'm not even remotely attracted to men who don't like women, especially ones who manhandle innocent girls in game parks.'

'I have already apologised for that unfortunate incident,' Nico told her in a bland, cold voice. 'And for your information, I won't have my well-ordered existence upset by some devious, impertinent female with a spectacular body and big violet eyes.'

By this time, Nico was becoming quite light-headed. He ushered Marianne into the hall, tossed her suitcase on to the floor and issued an instruction to the waiting Jeremiah to carry it to the guest room. He felt utterly weary. He closed his eyes briefly and ran a hand through his dark hair. The gesture fascinated Marianne, so that she stared openly.

His temples, she noted, were threaded attractively with silver. Fine lines of fatigue etched his eyes and mouth. His expression was remote, yet there was a touch of vulnerability which tugged at her emotions. She was conscious of a peculiar sensation, which she didn't have time to analyse.

Marianne had never seen anyone so large and rugged, with such vast shoulders. Slim hips lengthened into a pair of strong, muscular legs, moulded by the khaki material of his trousers. He wore sturdy brown leather boots, an expensive gold watch and the air of a man who had been goaded beyond all reasonable limits.

'I have no intention of disrupting your life,' Marianne snapped, albeit untruthfully.

'Good,' Nico replied coldly.

He stood gazing at her inscrutably from his great height.

'At least we understand each other.'

And that, Nico thought fiercely, was how it was going to stay!

3

Nico showed Marianne to her room and went to take a shower while Jeremiah, showing no curiosity whatever about the lady who had apparently arrived to stay, put the finishing touches to the meal.

Jeremiah had been sulky for days, and it was obvious that he was anxious to go to his own quarters where his disgruntled wife, Jemima, awaited him. Jemima, who made no secret of the fact that she disliked living on the reserve, reluctantly undertook to do the housework and laundry for Nico twice a week.

Suppressing a sigh, Nico told Jeremiah he could go off duty once the covered dishes had been placed on the sideboard. He would definitely have to give some thought in the near future to replacing his most unsuitable domestic staff.

Marianne gazed around the large dining-room in delight. Dr Logan might not like women, but he certainly knew what pleased them! Any woman would be more than happy to live in this type of luxury. There was an impressive Persian carpet on the dark, tiled floor. Its richness echoed the colour of the walls and reminded her of rubies and sapphires scattered on the floor of a sultan's tent.

There was gleaming silverware on the well-polished mahogany table and elegant, deeply-buttoned leather chairs surrounding it. One ruby wall was covered by gilt-framed portraits of large, dignified Victorian gentlemen with their smug, well-corseted wives. An ornate, glass-fronted rosewood cabinet filled with crystal ware and antique porcelain stood against the other wall, and a large silver candelabra graced the sideboard.

'You live in some style, Doctor Logan,' Marianne commented. 'I expected to find a rustic rondavel with mud walls and a dung floor.'

Despite the pain in his head and the fact that he had taken a strong dislike to his unwanted house guest, Nico replied politely.

'I am sorry to disappoint you, Miss Chattan.'

'Oh, I'm not disappointed in the least, just surprised.'

'Are you? We South African men like our creature comforts,' he mocked. 'We like shoes on our feet and a decent bed to sleep on. We're quite fond of wearing clothes, too. And we've long since given up the practice of eating one another.'

Marianne blushed.

'I didn't mean to imply that you were a bunch of savages.'

His firm mouth twitched.

'I'm relieved to hear it.'

Quickly Marianne changed the subject.

'Are those your ancestors?'

'Indeed they are. Two of them were Dutch and the other one came from Scotland. All doctors. I broke with tradition and took up veterinary medicine instead.'

Marianne had a sudden urge to know more about him, but she quelled it firmly. All she really needed to discover was what the man's weaknesses were. It was good strategy to discover the enemy's weak points in order to gain the upper hand in the battle.

Dr Logan, however, did not appear to have any weak points. He appeared to be strong in mind as well as in body. He was also extremely attractive, a fact she hadn't bargained for. If she wasn't careful she'd be in big trouble! Marianne unfolded her table napkin and frowned thoughtfully.

It was perfectly natural for a girl to be curious about any handsome man who crossed her path, but she would simply take great care not to succumb to his charm. Her plans had been carefully laid and she must not jeopardise them.

They began the first course, a rather watery potato soup not at all to Marianne's liking. Dr Logan's cook appeared never to have heard of condiments, she thought in disgust. Nico, watching her lazily from beneath half-closed eyes, noted the shudder and suppressed a grin.

'James told me that you were married at one time,' Marianne remarked casually, peeping at him from beneath her dark lashes, knowing the question was unforgivably rude, but she continued daringly, 'Do you live here alone?'

It seemed important to discover if there would be any opposition in her bid for his attentions. James hadn't mentioned anything about a girlfriend. He'd told her quite a lot, though, about the reprehensible Dr Logan, and if all he'd said about his half-brother were true, then it was little wonder the wife had walked out!

A stony mask descended over Nico's features. He had no time for nosy females.

'James is a mine of useless information,' he said in a cold, bland voice.

Marianne, stunned at the sudden

bleakness she had glimpsed in his eyes, decided to refrain from any further questions for the time being. Dr Logan's past wasn't really her business, anyway. It was his future which interested her! Tearing her eyes from his, she lifted her knife and fork and began to eat.

Jeremiah's stew was worse than usual. Nico watched Marianne coping valiantly with the tough meat and half-cooked vegetables and once more concealed his amusement. Serve the woman right! She'd invited herself into his home and she would have to abide by the consequences.

'Would you care for dessert, Miss Chattan?' he offered blandly.

Marianne looked up doubtfully.

'What is it?'

'It's bread pudding,' he explained, hoping to goodness Jeremiah hadn't used last week's mouldy bread. 'I don't particularly recommend it.'

'I'll pass,' Marianne said firmly.

'Then you won't mind if I go ahead?'

Nico helped himself liberally. He was a large male with a healthy appetite and any dessert was better than none.

'Oh, not at all,' Marianne assured him graciously.

The man could devour the whole bowl, for all she cared. He obviously had no idea whatever about decent food, a situation she intended to rectify. She had no intention of enduring this type of fare for the next few weeks, or however long it took to get Nicholas Logan hooked.

As to his unwillingness to let her stay under his roof for more than one night, she would simply have to change his mind for him, wouldn't she? She had the next twelve hours to think of something. However, Marianne was saved the trouble.

By midnight, Dr Logan was in no fit state to notice anything, let alone make any decisions. He was tossing about in his bed, his pulse alarmingly rapid. There was a fierce ache in his joints and he was sweating profusely.

'Malaria,' he muttered to himself, staggering to the bathroom for a glass of water.

He gulped it down thirstily, made his way back to bed and in the process, knocked over his bedside lamp. Then with an angry exclamation he slumped heavily across the bed and passed out.

Marianne, lying sleepless as she pondered her own problems, heard the commotion. She flung on her dressing-gown and slippers, hurried down the passage and flung open the door.

'What is it?' she gasped.

She could see nothing in the darkness, and groped for the light switch. Nico, in a state of near delirium, muttered incoherently. He wore nothing but a pair of navy sleeping shorts, and his physique was awesome. Marianne stared in fascination at the bare chest and arms, glistening with perspiration. As she watched, his whole body convulsed in a shivering fit.

'You're ill!' she squealed in alarm. 'Why didn't you call me?'

Returning to the kitchen, she found a bowl of tepid water and set about gently sponging his face and torso in an attempt to bring down the fever. Struggling to shift his inert body into a better position left her red with exertion, after which she found a blanket with which to cover him. His breathing, she noted in alarm, was rather shallow. Nico groaned, still muttering feverishly.

'Have you taken any medication for your flu?' she asked, not really expecting an answer.

Nico opened his eyes and tried to focus on her face.

'C-c-cold.'

'Yes, I know.'

Marianne, a soft-hearted girl, flung aside all reserve.

'Turn over,' she said, and gave his shoulder a shove.

With a groan Nico obeyed. Marianne switched off the light, kicked off her slippers and slid under the blanket beside him. With one arm around his waist she curved her body into his, allowing her heat to warm him. Eventually she felt Nico relax. He stopped shivering and gave a deep sigh.

'Carina?'

Marianne stiffened.

'No, it's not Carina, it's Marianne.'

'Nice hair,' he murmured, and fell into a restless sleep.

Who, Marianne wondered, was Carina? An unaccountable shaft of pure jealousy ripped through her, leaving her stunned. She had no reason to feel this way, and even less right!

As soon as Nico was breathing evenly she attempted to withdraw her arm, intending to creep back to her own bedroom. She did not relish the embarrassment of being caught in his bed once he was awake. Nico stirred, turned over and held her fast, so that her cheek was pressed against one large shoulder.

Marianne gave a resigned sigh. There was no way she could escape now without waking him up. She allowed her eyelids to drift closed. It was warm and cosy in Nico's bed and his large body felt solid and reassuring. She'd stay for another few minutes.

She awakened a few hours later to such an amazing cascade of sound that it took a moment for her to realise what it was — the dawn chorus. Birdsong in Africa, Marianne marvelled, was an indescribable delight! She lay for a few moments trying to identify the birds, but gave up in frustration, determined to find a book on South African birds when she next visited a bookstore.

Creeping from Nico's bed to her own bedroom, Marianne showered quickly and dressed before finding her way to the kitchen for a cup of coffee and a sketchy breakfast of toast and marmalade. When she returned, Nico was tossing about in a fevered stare, muttering about someone called Jenna.

Marianne frowned. One of his women friends, perhaps? She would have to ascertain as soon as possible

whether there were any serious con-
tenders for his affections, and if so,
develop a strategy to outshine them.
She had a mission to accomplish, the
Chattan honour to avenge, had she not?

Nico, completely unaware of her
ministrations as she attempted to
sponge him down, slept fitfully for most
of the following day, awakening at
intervals for brief drinks of water. When
there was no sign of the fever and
shivering fits abating, Marianne began
to realise that Dr Logan was far more ill
than she had at first surmised. She went
into the kitchen, intent on questioning
a reluctant Jeremiah.

At her approach, Nico's cook turned
from the stove and presented her with a
sulky face.

'Do you know if there is a doctor in
the area, Jeremiah?' she asked.

Jeremiah shook his head.

'Dr Carina, she go away,' he
informed her in his broken English.
'She not like it here at Matonga.'

'I see.'

So that's who Carina was — Nicholas Logan's ex-wife, and a doctor by profession. She must be the woman James had spoken of, the one he'd helped to rescue from her intolerable marriage.

'Is there any other doctor nearby?'

Jeremiah shook his head.

'No doctor here in Matonga.'

Marianne decided not to take his word for it, but drive to Sunrise Lodge in the next valley as soon as possible. Surely someone there would be able to tell her where to find a doctor. Nico needed medical attention without delay. She went to the bedroom once more, and satisfied that he was still asleep, let herself quietly out of the house where an indifferent Jeremiah showed her how to operate the remote control mechanism for the gate.

Feeling a little uncertain, Marianne drove past the whitewashed offices and out of the immediate enclosure, into the body of the reserve. The road wound through a vast area of tawny grassland, dotted randomly with weirdly-shaped thorn trees.

She gasped as a herd of springbok bounded over the road in front of the car, forcing her to apply the brakes rather sharply. Her dismay soon turned to fascination as she watched the animals springing away in graceful arcs across the veldt. Yesterday's rain had obviously provided a welcome relief from the suffocating heat, and in the distance she glimpsed a waterhole where zebra and impala were quietly drinking.

Rounding a corner, Marianne let out a small squeal of fright and hastily applied the brakes once more. She stared in awe at a herd of elephant, including several youngsters, which stood in the middle of the road, ears flapping and trunks waving. She had never been this close to the world's largest land animal before, and it was a rather scary experience. Tentatively she sounded the horn, but the animals took not the slightest notice.

'Well, you may have nothing to do,' she scolded them, 'but I am on an important assignment. Your boss is ill, and I need to get help.'

When they still did not respond to this entreaty Marianne put her head out of the window and yelled.

'Move it!'

To her amazement, the leader, a huge male, eyed her placidly and trundled off obediently into the grass, to be followed by the rest of the herd. With a sigh of relief Marianne revved the engine and sped off up the hill. At the main gates she waved to the uniformed guard and turned left on to the tarred road in the direction of Sunrise Lodge.

It was early as yet and the dense vegetation on either side of the road was wet with dew. Through the electric fence, inside the reserve, she noticed a lone giraffe standing sentinel under a tree, and thought she had never seen anything more beautiful. Lofty and elegant, he deliberately selected the best leaves from the top of the tree and gave her a coquettish glance as he chewed them.

Marianne's heart was lost. How delightful it must be to live permanently in this part of the world! If she lived here she would never tire of watching the multi-faceted wonder of it all. For a moment she almost wished that her bogus forthcoming engagement to Dr Nicholas Logan wasn't bogus at all, a futile thought!

Ten minutes down the road, Marianne came upon a signpost advertising Sunrise Lodge. She slowed the car and turned through a pair of tall gateposts which heralded a long, winding drive, only to discover that the rambling whitewashed building at the end of it was a total delight.

She parked on the irrigated emerald lawn and gazed at the thatched building before her. It had numerous low windows framed by scarlet bougainvillea bushes, salmon-coloured hibiscus and a variety of spring annuals. The perfume of the blossoms caused Marianne's senses to give a small leap of pleasure. Yes, this was a beautiful part of the world, and she would store up its beauties in her brain, to be taken out and examined when she was far away from it all, when she was an elderly spinster in a lonely bedsit, perhaps?

Marianne thrust aside these depressing thoughts along with her envy. Dr Logan and his compatriots were lucky indeed. She was quite sure that nothing would make her forget the tall, intriguing man in whose home she had stayed, or the wonderful surroundings she'd so briefly enjoyed.

The interior of the hotel was dark and cool. Marianne glanced around with interest, hoping as she rang the desk bell that someone would be available to help her. An elegant woman approached from the office, her high-heeled sandals tapping importantly on the polished floor.

She shot Marianne a swift look of appraisal and informed her dismissively, 'If you are looking for accommodation,

I'm afraid we are full. I suggest you try the Ratanga Inn, about twenty miles farther on.'

'Good morning,' Marianne greeted her, politely but pointedly.

If this was the way the woman greeted all her guests, it was a wonder she was still in business! On closer inspection she was not quite as young as Marianne had first surmised, but was beautifully made-up, with a shining cap of blonde hair, quite obviously not natural.

'I'm not looking for a room, I'm looking for a doctor,' Marianne continued. 'Can you tell me where to find one, please?'

'A doctor? Good heavens, we are not a hospital, you know.'

Marianne hid her irritation.

'I realise that. All I'm asking for is information.'

'Then you'll have to try Krugerville, our nearest town. Dr Bester and partners have a surgery there. You're obviously not from these parts, so I suppose I shall have to explain. Krugerville's about half an hour's drive past the Ratanga Inn. Stay on this road and you shouldn't have a problem.'

'Thank you.'

'Is it urgent?'

'Yes. Someone from the Matonga Reserve is in need of medical attention.'

The woman's gaze narrowed sharply.

'Matonga? Who's ill?'

'The veterinarian.'

'Nico? The poor man! Why didn't you say so? What's the problem?'

Marianne considered if to be none of the woman's business.

'I'm not sure,' she hedged.

'I'm Davina Delahunt, the owner here,' the woman informed her in a suddenly gracious voice. 'I'll telephone the surgery for you, if you like,' and disappeared into the office.

A moment later she re-emerged with the news that a Dr David Bester would call to see Dr Logan at midday. Before Marianne could thank her, Mrs Delahunt waded in with her questions.

'What are you doing at Matonga? Nico said nothing to me about any female visitors. How long are you staying? What's your name?'

'Marianne Chattan.'

'Are you staying in the hutted camp?'

'No. I'm a house guest.'

This piece of news did not appear to please Mrs Delahunt at all.

'I see.'

She looked Marianne up and down.

'I'm frightfully busy but you can tell Nico that I'll be across to see him just as soon as I can.'

'I doubt he'll be up to socialising much,' Marianne pointed out. 'He isn't very well.'

Mrs Delahunt smiled sweetly, a knowing glint in her green eyes.

'Oh, I wouldn't worry about that, my dear. Nico is always pleased to see me.'

Marianne drove back to Matonga as quickly as she dared and hurried into the bedroom only to find that Nico was still asleep, sprawled across the bed, having flung off the blanket. One arm trailed down to the floor, his long fingers curled relaxedly in sleep. Gently Marianne lifted the arm, took his pulse, and laid it on the bed. The pulse was far too rapid. When she attempted to cover him up, he muttered angrily.

'Go away.'

'OK, OK, I'm going!' Marianne told him.

There was nothing more she could do for the moment, so she went into the kitchen in search of something to drink.

The sun was staring brassily out of an azure sky when she found a shady spot on the vine-covered patio in order to sip her iced tea. It was time to take stock of the situation and plan her next move. There was very little she could do with Dr Logan so obviously laid up. It was frustrating, but she would have to be patient.

As Marianne mused, a shiny green sunbird alighted on a nearby bush and poked its long beak into a trumpet-shaped red flower in order to sip the nectar. Fascinated, she sat very still and watched. When the bird disappeared she gave a small sigh of regret. This place was getting to her. If she wasn't careful she'd start wanting to stay on at Matonga indefinitely, and that simply would not do.

It might be an enchanting little piece of heaven but there was another world out there, one she'd have to return to just as soon as she'd accomplished what she'd set out to do — which was to avenge Logan treachery.

However, it was to be hoped that she could stay here for some time yet because there was so much animal life she still wanted to see!

True to his word, Dr David Bester arrived at midday in his green Range Rover. He was a tall, fair young man, obviously on the best of terms with his patient. He examined Nico thoroughly and rejoined Marianne in the hall.

'Malaria,' he informed her succinctly. 'I've given him an injection and I will call again tomorrow with some capsules. I've prescribed a very effective drug, so see that he takes it, will you? Give him plenty of fluids and keep him as comfortable as possible. With some good nursing he should be on his feet again in about two weeks' time.'

He shot Marianne a curious glance.

'Are you a friend of Nico's, Miss Chattan?'

Marianne went pink.

'Er . . . yes, I'm a friend.'

The doctor studied her face.

'I see. You'll take good care of him, won't you? He's a decent chap, and he's doing a wonderful job here at Matonga.'

Marianne assured the doctor that she would do her best. As to whether she really was a friend, that remained to be seen, but if all went according to plan she would very soon be a lot more than a friend. She'd be his ever-loving fiancée!

She gave a secret, triumphant smile as she ushered the doctor out. If she played her cards right, Nicholas Logan, half-brother of the detestable James

Logan, would fall for her within weeks. Thereafter it would be a simple matter to lead him up the garden path, as it were, exactly what James had done to her!

Jeremiah was waiting for her in the kitchen. As soon as he saw her he gave a grunt and tossed his keys on to the counter.

'Jemima and I, we go, now,' he informed her sulkily.

Marianne looked blank.

'Go where?'

'To our home. Jemima, she not like it here. She like the township better, so we not work here any more. Jemima say you can cook for the boss now.'

Marianne's heart sank.

'I'll relay the message, Jeremiah.'

Jeremiah, now that he'd arranged things to his satisfaction, disappeared without another word.

'Well!' Marianne snorted. 'Just like that! I suppose I shall have to shoulder all the housework as well, not to mention the laundry.'

Then she gave a slow smile. The departure of Jeremiah and his wife could be the very thing she needed to further her aims. She'd keep Nico's house pristine, cook him wonderful meals and generally make herself so indispensable that he'd offer her a housekeeping job. It was a far cry from veterinary nursing, but it would only be for a few weeks.

Dr Bester arrived the following day with the promised medication and from then on Nico began to improve almost hourly. Marianne took care to nurse him meticulously for the next week, giving him plenty of drinks and ensuring that he was kept comfortable. By the end of the week, he was taking a little food, mainly nourishing broths which she had painstakingly concocted in Jeremiah's kitchen where she had discovered the unpleasant fact that the cupboards were in a state. She was forced to spend an entire morning cleaning and putting them to rights.

On Monday morning, Nico took a

shower, donned a clean set of khaki bush clothes, fastened on his sturdy boots and presented himself in the kitchen for breakfast. He looked drawn and tired and had lost weight, but was nonetheless in perfect command of the situation. Marianne turned from frying bacon and gaped at him.

'What are you doing here? You're supposed to be in bed!'

His eyebrows rose.

'I intend to take a drive through the reserve.'

'You'll do no such thing,' Marianne told him firmly. 'You look as though you're about to expire.'

'And you sound like a nagging wife.'

He eyed her inscrutably from his great height.

'Why are you cooking the breakfast?'

'I'm cooking because if I don't, we'd both starve, that's why!'

She smiled suddenly.

'Besides, I like cooking.'

'Is that so?'

'You bet. I bake bread, cakes, scones,

you-name-it, and I have a mean recipe for chilli.'

Nico's eyes glinted.

'Then feel free to use my kitchen as often as you wish, Miss Chattan, but clear it with Jeremiah first. And on no account, I beg of you, serve any blancmange.'

'Done,' Marianne agreed.

Hiding her satisfaction, she ladled bacon and eggs on to the plates.

'Why do you wish to gallivant when you are obviously in no condition to do so?'

Nico folded his large body on to a chair. The woman was a complete nosy-parker, but she'd been very kind to him all week so he would satisfy her curiosity, for what the information was worth.

He said coolly, 'I need to instruct some of my staff, and there are one or two matters to check on. What's it to you?'

'Well, I promised Dr Bester that I'd take good care of you.'

She slapped a plate in front of him and added firmly, 'You are to get back into bed as soon as you have eaten, and I mean that! You look as though you have one of those nice brown leather boots of yours in a pine box already.'

Nico allowed himself a faint grin.

'You exaggerate.'

'No, I don't. Anyway, you have no need to go sniffing around the reserve, you know. Your staffing situation is well under control, and everybody appears to know exactly what they have to do this week. They have even clubbed together to buy the boss a massive basket of fruit, which should be arriving from Krugerville at midday, all wrapped up, with a red bow, or so I am reliably informed.'

Nico gaped.

'How do you know all this?'

Oh, I make it my business to pop into the office from time to time. The warden with the red hair said I was to tell you that he had everything strictly under control, and you are not to concern yourself. Your deputy, I think he said he was.'

Nico said slowly, 'I have misjudged you, Miss Chattan. You appear to have gone to a lot of trouble on my behalf.'

'It was a pleasure. Now, will you kindly get back into bed?'

'Is that an invitation?'

Marianne's eyes flashed.

'Certainly not!'

He was laughing at her behind that bland expression, she just knew it, and her cheeks became even pinker.

'It's lonely in bed.'

'Tough.'

Nico helped himself to another slice of toast.

'You're a hard, unfeeling female, Miss Chattan, and I don't know why I allow you to remain in my home.'

'I do. You need a cleaning woman, a laundress and a cook. Your erstwhile domestic help has deserted you,' Marianne informed him with relish.

Nico's head snapped up.

'Jeremiah's gone?'

'So it seems. He said his wife didn't like it here. It doesn't look as though he did, either. They won't be back, so you'll have to find replacements. In the meantime,' she said sweetly, 'while I'm in your home, I'm glad to help.'

Nico's face emptied of all expression.

'Ah, yes, the little matter of your accommodation, Miss Chattan. I seem to recall that I had asked you to leave.'

His voice turned steely.

'You may remain just as long as it takes for me to find another cook.'

'And then?'

'You'll be hitting the road, toad, as they say.'

He looked so pleased at the prospect that Marianne's temper erupted.

'When I do hit the road, Doctor Logan, the pleasure will be all mine, believe me! And let me jog your memory. If it hadn't been for me, buster, you'd be lying on a slab by now.'

Nico surveyed her inscrutably over the rim of his coffee mug.

'You're exaggerating again.'

'I am not!' Marianne flared.

'Don't think,' he said silkily, 'that I'm not grateful for what you've done. I am indeed indebted to you.'

For some reason, that remark pleased Marianne greatly. She favoured him with one of her best smiles, so that Nico's eyes darkened to slate.

'You'll leave as soon as it can be arranged,' he growled, 'and I shall reimburse you suitably for your trouble.'

The woman was getting to him Big Time in more ways than one, he reflected. The sooner she took herself out of his life, the better. He liked her bossy little ways and the sassy manner which hid, he suspected, an inner vulnerability which she tried her utmost to hide. He also liked the way her smile made the whole world seem a brighter place.

Annoyed at his thoughts, Nico gulped down his coffee and stood up, a little too quickly it seemed, for the next moment he found himself flat on his back on the hard kitchen floor. Marianne giggled.

'Oh, dear,' she smirked, 'you're not quite as fit as you think you are, are you?'

With a rueful grin Nico hauled himself to his feet.

'It seems not. I think I'll just take myself back to bed, as you suggest.'

Marianne felt a sneaking sympathy as she watched him go. The man was really quite endearing. It was a great pity he was related to that obnoxious jerk, James Logan. Thoughtfully Marianne chewed her toast.

If she'd met Nico Logan at any other time she would have been quite smitten, it was useless to deny it. As it was, she'd had to be on her guard all week against her treacherous emotions. She loved Nico's foreign-sounding accent and those incredible grey eyes. They were smoky at one moment and as cold as steel the next. But to fall for the man now was just not on. She must remember why she was here. Her plans had been most carefully laid and she would not allow them to be changed!

Marianne rose and began to place the used crockery into the dishwasher. Things were progressing very nicely indeed, albeit slowly. It was gratifying that Dr Logan was beginning to feel some attraction for her. She'd seen it in his eyes. She would keep him at arm's length for a while and then turn on a little more charm, all the while being extremely careful not to wade in too deep.

She gave a bitter little smile as she activated the dishwasher, glancing at her empty ring finger as she did so. There was a tell-tale white mark where James's flashy diamonds had lain. Diamonds were said to be a girl's best friend, and soon she'd be wearing another one. Unlike most girls, though, the thought left Marianne feeling positively wretched.

4

The promised basket of fruit arrived at midday, and hot on the heels of the delivery van came Davina Delahunt's shiny yellow sports car. She breezed into the house without waiting to be admitted and informed a startled Marianne, 'I'm here to see Nico.'

Incensed at the woman's rudeness, Marianne led her down the passage. Whatever the relationship between Nico Logan and this woman, there was such a thing as good manners!

Nico looked up from the veterinary journal he was attempting to read. His face went carefully blank.

'Good morning, Davina.'

'Nico, darling. I've left a little dish of egg custard in the kitchen for you. I had our chef make it especially, so see that you eat it,' Davina told him bossily.

Marianne, standing in the doorway,

was pleased to notice Nico's suppressed shudder. He thanked Davina politely, hiding his impatience. Three weeks ago it was a new tie, the month before that a subscription to a magazine he had no intention of reading, and today it was a dish of muck. The woman was a confounded nuisance.

'You'll stay for a cup of coffee?' he offered, gesturing towards an armchair near the window.

Davina ignored the armchair, perching instead on his bed. She laid a proprietary hand on his thigh and smiled coquettishly,

'My poor darling, you must be feeling grim. Why didn't you call on me earlier? Not that I'd have been able to drop everything at a moment's notice, you understand. I'm frightfully busy at present.'

She shot Marianne a look of intense dislike.

'This young woman came knocking on my door for help and of course I telephoned David Bester immediately.

Who is she, anyway?'

'Miss Marianne Chattan is my
. . . new housekeeper,' Nico supplied
smoothly. 'Marianne, may I introduce
my neighbour, Mrs Davina Delahunt?'

For some reason Nico's referring to
her as his housekeeper irked Marianne,
and yet that was effectively what she
was, for the moment, at any rate!

'Did you say housekeeper?' Davina
queried sharply, her beautiful mouth
curved in a sneer. 'You distinctly told
me you were a house guest, Miss
Chattan. Getting a little above yourself,
aren't you?'

Marianne's cheeks reddened.

'My exact position in this household
has nothing whatever to do with you,
Mrs Delahunt,' she observed sweetly.

Nico concealed his amusement and
asked blandly, 'Would you be so kind as
to make my guest a cup of coffee,
Marianne?'

Marianne's face darkened further.

'Coming right up, sir,' she snapped,
emphasising the 'sir'.

A few moments later she returned with a tray and was forced to suppress a strong desire to accidentally spill the coffee all over Davina Delahunt's pristine linen suit. She was being childish, she knew, but there was something about Nico Logan and his affairs which evoked very strong feelings inside her. It was bewildering.

Davina accepted a cup of coffee without bothering to thank her.

'We have some interesting guests staying at the lodge, Nico. They have expressed a wish to experience a safari so I advised them to contact your office.'

She gave a tinkling laugh.

'I hope you realise that I'm always promoting Matonga.'

'Your guests will have to book quickly,' Nico observed. 'I am told that we are almost full for the next month.'

'Pooh! Your wardens will do anything to oblige me. I send Matonga plenty of custom, after all.'

'That may be so but we only have a

certain number of vacancies and it's first come, first served.'

'Even so, my guests are important,' Davina insisted arrogantly. 'They're here to take photographs for a prestigious travel magazine and the photographer is a most impressive young man from London, charming, and so good looking! He wishes to take a trophy of some sort back to England, to show his friends, lion or elephant, it doesn't particularly matter. I told them that you'd organise something. After all, you're always killing your animals, aren't you, darling? What's one more dead beast when you have so many on the reserve?'

Nico's face darkened.

He told her shortly, 'I am quite prepared to cull an animal or two when absolutely necessary, in fact, you know as well as I do that it is imperative, to prevent over-population in the reserve by matching the number of animals with the available food supply. But I refuse to allow the mindless, wanton destruction of animals in order to feed

96

the egos of a few selfish tourists. You may tell your guests that they are welcome to take photographs, but there will be no shooting.'

Davina looked sulky for a moment and then thought better of it.

'No problem, darling. You're ill and just a teensy bit irritable.'

No doubt he'd be in a better mood when her guests were ready for that safari. She'd speak to him about it again later.

Nico finished his coffee, lay back on the pillows and closed his eyes. He wished to goodness the woman would take herself off. He'd never felt so exhausted in his life.

Marianne, taking her cue, began to collect up the cups.

'Dr Logan needs to rest now, Mrs Delahunt,' she said sweetly. 'Thank you for the custard. I shall see you out.'

Davina stood up, her colour high.

'I shall see myself out, Miss Chattan.'

Her high-heeled sandals tapped sharply on the kitchen floor.

'I shall be back to visit Nico,' she flung over her shoulder, 'and next time you shall remain at the sink, where you belong!'

Marianne closed the door firmly, relieved to see the back of Nico's unpleasant visitor. For some reason the thought of a relationship between the two of them set her teeth on edge, which was ridiculous because Dr Logan's private life had nothing what-soever to do with her, at least not until after she'd had her wicked way with him.

A small voice told her that it may not be as easy as she had imagined. He wasn't the type of man to be swayed by a pretty face or an arch manner, or a few kisses, for that matter. He struck her as being a man who lived his life by principle, not the emotion of the moment. With a heartfelt sigh she set about making an appetising macaroni cheese dish for lunch. She garnished it carefully with strips of crispy bacon and tiny triangles of fried bread. Adding

Davina's egg custard to the tray with the hope that Nico would choke on it, she took it down the passage.

'You are turning into an unpleasant little shrew, Marianne,' she muttered ruefully.

She would be heartily glad when this whole business was over and she could revert to being pleasant, honest little Miss Chattan again. Her thoughts turned to Inchfarrel and the sleepy village of her birth. She missed her friends and family but in the short time she had spent in this beautiful country she had undergone a subtle yet profound change. How would she ever be able to live anywhere else?

As she entered the room Nico tossed his magazine aside and cast an appreciative eye over the tray.

'Join me please, Marianne.'

Surprised, Marianne went to fetch her own tray from the kitchen and settled into the armchair next to the window. The macaroni, she was pleased to note, was a huge success. Nico complimented her after the first mouthful and for the first time in days appeared to have regained his appetite, eating with unconcealed enjoyment.

'You really can cook,' he murmured disbelievingly. 'What else can you do, I wonder.'

'Oh, pretty well anything,' Marianne informed him airily.

'I must remember that.'

She refilled his cup with coffee from the silver pot she'd brought from the kitchen. As she handed it to him, Nico's fingers closed around her wrist.

'Stay and talk to me a while, Marianne.'

Marianne looked at him warily.

'What about?'

'Oh, this and that. How do you like Matonga?'

Nico's voice was casual, at odds with the intent look in his eyes.

'You don't find it too tedious, living here? It's a very quiet life we lead.'

Marianne set the tray to one side and perched on the bed, her face alight with enthusiasm.

'It's quiet, yes, but I find it wonderfully satisfying. It's a marvellous place for people, especially those from the city, to experience nature and leave the rat race behind. I imagine that you'd get to know who you are again. A person could live here for years and years and never become bored, especially if one is living with . . . '

She broke off in horror at what she'd been about to say.

'With?'

'Well, the right person . . . I mean . . . present company excluded, of course. I'm not referring to us.'

Nico's eyes glinted.

'Quite. You would not miss the bright lights? A girl like you needs theatres and boutiques and restaurants.'

Marianne considered for a moment.

'I've never lived like that, quite honestly. I was brought up in a tiny village where we made our own entertainment, with the occasional visit to Inverness or Edinburgh. I daresay it would be fun to hit the high spots once in a while with the right person, like I said, but it would soon pall if you had to do it all the time, believe me.'

Missing his look of surprise, she enthused on.

'You are fortunate to live in the African bush, Nico. It's a harsh life out here, but a vibrant one. One feels so very . . . alive! And there's peace here.'

Her eyes widened in sudden discovery.

'Yes, there really is peace here.'

Much of her inner turmoil had dissipated in the past days, Marianne reflected. What's more, she hadn't thought about James in days.

Nico continued to regard her over the rim of his coffee cup. How could a girl like Marianne Chattan understand so completely after less than two weeks?

'I could stay here for ever,' Marianne murmured dreamily, amazed to discover that she really meant it.

A gleam appeared in Nico's grey eyes, to be quickly damped down.

'That's interesting.'

He cleared his throat.

'I agree, there is a lot here for a person to discover, but once you've discovered it all, what then?'

'Then you continue to live here and enjoy it. End of story. And a very happy end of story, that would be, too.'

'You really mean that?'

'Yes.'

Her violet eyes sparked with excitement.

'Take that herd of springbok on the road the other day. They were totally wonderful, with their red-brown coats and the white markings flashing like banners in the sun. How could you ever, ever not enjoy a sight like that, even though you've seen it a hundred times?'

Unaware that Nico was a world authority on antelope, she enquired if he'd noticed the creatures.

'Indeed, I have,' he told her gravely, adding casually, 'Those white patterns serve to reflect solar radiation, which helps the animal to keep cool in the heat. In a really dry climate they don't need much water, either. They extract their moisture from the plants they eat.'

'Really? How fascinating,' Marianne exclaimed. 'The springbok is your country's national emblem, isn't it? How high can it spring?'

'About two metres. When there's danger about, their jumping signals a warning, and confuses the enemy.'

Nico studied her face and said slowly, 'I had no idea you were this interested in our wildlife, Marianne.'

'I have always been fascinated with birds and animals of every description,' she assured him fervently. 'That's why I became a veterinary nurse in the first place. It seemed the next best thing to actually living in a wild place like this.'

'You really are a veterinary nurse? I thought . . . '

'You thought I was lying?'

'Well, yes, to be frank. It seems I have misjudged you considerably.'

He smiled and she smiled back, suddenly aware of a warm feeling in the region of her heart. Her smile disappeared when he asked abruptly, 'How long have you known James Logan?'

Marianne looked away quickly.

'About a year.'

She had no wish to be reminded of how James Logan with his London sophistication and big-city ways had swept a naïve country girl off her feet. She wished she'd never met the man!

'What does James mean to you?'

Hastily Marianne gathered up the tray. This conversation was becoming a little uncomfortable.

'Nothing.'

She was both surprised and relieved to find that it was true, and her eyes darkened to indigo.

She repeated clearly, 'Absolutely nothing!'

Nico let out the breath he had been holding.

'Thank you for a delightful lunch, Marianne. I enjoyed it very much.'

He was leaning his large shoulders against the headboard, gazing with interest at her suddenly pink cheeks. He looked solid and safe and extremely handsome, and Marianne's heartbeat tripled its rhythm. With mumbled thanks she turned and bore the tray to the kitchen. The African bush and Nicholas Logan together were a heady combination, and she would have to be extremely careful in future. Under no circumstances must she allow herself to fall under the spell of either of them.

★ ★ ★

Nico had been back at work for a full week before he came home for lunch and informed her, 'I would like to take you out to dinner this evening.'

Marianne, hiding sudden confusion, placed a steaming bowl of soup before him. Her normally husky voice took on a squeaky quality.

'Why?'

If he was surprised at the forthright question, Nico concealed it.

'I wish to thank you for the way you

nursed me back to health.'

'Oh.'

She smiled at him kindly.

'There's no need, you know. I'd have done it for anyone.'

Her tone implied, any sick animal, that is . . .

'Nevertheless, you will oblige me by being ready at six-thirty.'

He was using the kind of voice an employer would use with an employee and she didn't much care to disobey. With outward meekness and secret annoyance, she agreed. At least it meant she wouldn't have to produce a meal tonight.

Nico had been very appreciative of her cooking during the past week, and at the knowledge Marianne felt a little glow under her ribs. She'd kept his home looking pristine, too. The amazing thing was that she found herself enjoying every minute of her day, including the brief times she sat out on the patio with a cup of tea, inhaling the scents of the surrounding bush and enjoying the rich variety of bird life which found its way into the garden.

The highlight for her had been the evenings when Nico had taken her for short drives through the reserve, explaining his work. She'd been fascinated to see the numerous kinds of game and was amazed at the competent and scientific way they were managed.

On one occasion they had discovered an orphaned hartebeest calf resting against the perimeter fence. It was in a dehydrated state, not having fed for a number of days. Gently Nico had lifted the small antelope into the jeep, admitted it to Matonga's sick bay behind one of the offices, and instructed a warden to feed it with baby milk from a bottle.

'Use a small teat,' Marianne had heard him say. 'Four-hourly feeds. I'll examine him again in the morning.'

She had been extremely impressed with the facility and harboured a secret yearning to work there. She would suggest it later on, when Nico had found a replacement housekeeper. Marianne went to the bathroom to wash her hair. If she was going out to dinner, she might as well make herself look presentable. She had brought only one suitable dress with her and it would have to do. It was a burgundy velvet with long, tight sleeves and a scooped neckline. She brushed out her long, silky hair and hastily fastened it into an elaborate coil at her neck, unaware that she looked quite beautiful.

Nico came in from his work, gave her a long, appraising stare and said simply, 'I won't be long.'

He re-emerged fifteen minutes later, looking superb in a dinner jacket. Marianne hid her admiration. He was incredibly sophisticated, a man of the world. Whoever would have thought he spent his days in the bush? She strove for composure and almost achieved it.

'This is the only dress I have with me, I'm afraid. I do hope we are not going anywhere grand.'

He smiled faintly.

'Out here? Hardly. I've booked a table at Sunrise Lodge, and you look very lovely tonight, Marianne.'

She thought she detected admiration in his eyes, and something else, something she couldn't quite define. Marianne went faintly pink.

'Thank you.'

She turned to pick up her small black evening bag, conscious of a feeling of disappointment that they should be dining at Davina Delahunt's establishment. Hopefully the woman would not interfere with them in any way.

Nico drove them to Sunrise Lodge in the silver Mercedes which Marianne had glimpsed in the garage on the day she'd arrived.

The restaurant section was furnished, surprisingly enough, with a restrained splendour. The table was laid with crystal ware, lace napkins and bone-handled cutlery. Whatever her faults, Marianne thought, Davina Delahunt had taste.

'If this isn't grand, I don't know what is,' she murmured ingenuously.

'It's not bad for the wilds of Africa,'

Nico conceded. 'May I suggest the giraffe liver pâté as a starter, followed by the ostrich steaks with baked apricots?'

Marianne looked up in alarm.

'I'm not used to eating things like that.'

'There is always a first time,' Nico contended gently, and an imp of mischief made him add, 'Of course, if you'd prefer it, there is also a choice of crocodile steak, roast elephant feet or stuffed porcupine with puff adder.'

'I'll have the ostrich,' Marianne told him quickly, not quite sure whether he was joking or not.

Nico hid a smile.

'Good girl. We'll make a South African of you yet.'

For some reason, that pleased Marianne very much.

Nico ordered an expensive wine.

'I think you'll like it.'

Marianne, who knew nothing of wines, sipped the plum-coloured liquid and agreed. Surprisingly, she found that she enjoyed the ostrich steak, too, followed by a delicious confection of cream, coconut milk and mango-flavoured ice-cream. They were drinking their coffee when Davina appeared at their table.

'Enjoying yourselves?' she asked, casting a bright, malicious glance in Marianne's direction. 'I daresay Miss Chattan is happy to be entertained by the boss this evening. It makes a change from working in the kitchen.'

The implication was that Marianne must not be allowed to forget her place. She was, after all, Nico's employee. Marianne wondered how a person who looked as beautiful as Mrs Delahunt could be so rude. She bit back an angry retort, refusing to give the woman the satisfaction of knowing how annoyed she was. Instead, she sat very upright and smiled, unaware that the beautiful red liquid she'd been consuming with such abandon was having its inevitable effect.

'Oh, we're enjoying ourselves all right,' she retorted, her tongue quite loosened, 'and you will be pleased to hear, Mrs Delahunt, that Dr Logan is not my boss.'

She leaned forward and spoke conspiratorially.

'He's now my fiancé,' she added with a hint of mischief.

Peeping at Nico from beneath her thick lashes, Marianne continued unsteadily.

'I'm going to marry you soon, aren't I, Nico, darling?'

She squinted in his direction as she endeavoured to gauge his reaction, but not a muscle on his face had moved. There was a long silence. Marianne, aware that she had said something momentous, fought a strong desire to giggle.

'Is this true?' Davina demanded of Nico, her lovely face distorted with ill-concealed fury.

Nico's mouth twitched. It was certainly a tempting offer — the answer to all his problems, in fact, and handed to him on a plate! If he married the delectable Miss Chattan he would have a mother for Jenna, no more harassment from Davina and unlimited, smashing desserts for the rest of his life! However, he was an honourable man, so he would be forced to decline. How could he take advantage of Miss Chattan in her present tipsy state?

He was also a gallant man. How could he let her down in her hour of need?

He said smoothly, 'You may have the pleasure of congratulating us, Davina. Since you are the first to know our happy news, we would ask you to keep it quiet for the moment. Perhaps we may have a bottle of your excellent champagne?'

Davina turned on her heel without another word and left. A moment later a harassed-looking wine waiter appeared with a tray and glasses, having endured the lash of his employer's tongue. Marianne, trying to focus on the hapless man, found her voice along with her pride.

'There was no need, Nico,' she hissed. 'It was only a joke.'

Nico poured the bubbly liquid into the glasses with every sign of pleasure.

'A toast to us, Marianne,' he told her silkily, his eyes intent above the rim of his glass, 'and there is every need. Davina is watching us from the doorway. We must keep up appearances, must we not?'

He touched his glass to hers.

'May we be as happy as a pair of warthogs in mud, and just as fruitful.'

Marianne choked.

'That wasn't necessary. You're despicable!'

'You're the one who started this. I wonder why.'

Marianne drained her glass, quite forgetful that it was not lemonade. The champagne on top of the quantity of wine she'd had with the meal did not help matters one little bit.

'I'm not used to drinking like this,' she told Nico crossly, 'which is no doubt the reason I said what I did just now, about marrying you, I mean. But now that it's all out in the open . . . '

She paused uncertainly, trying vainly to marshal her thoughts. She had to remember her plan! Something about getting him to the altar . . .

'Yes?' Nico encouraged, hiding his delight.

Marianne gave a small, unladylike hiccough.

'Will you marry me, Nico? Really marry me, I mean?'

Without hesitation Nico reached across the table and covered her hand with his.

'It would be a pleasure, Miss Chattan. I'm already in love with your hair.'

Marianne smiled mistily.

'Oh, good. Now I can relax. I've been wondering how I could get you to propose. You're quite a catch, you know.'

Nico laughed softly.

'I am taking you home now, my dear.'

He helped her from the table, took

her firmly by the arm and marched her from the restaurant. Once in the Mercedes, Marianne turned on her side, snuggled into his broad shoulder and promptly fell asleep.

Nico, nosing the Mercedes along the quiet road, ran a hand through his neat dark hair and settled back to think.

5

The sun was high in the sky by the time Marianne awoke, having slept heavily, oblivious even of the magnificent birdsong outside her window in the early hours of the morning. She sat up in bed, held her head in her hands and groaned. There was the vaguest memory of having made a complete fool of herself the previous evening, but with any luck Nico would have forgotten whatever it was she'd said to him.

There was a knock at the door.

'Come in,' she croaked.

Nico walked in with a steaming mug of coffee, his face carefully blank.

'You've surfaced at last, I see. How does the head feel?'

Marianne frowned heavily.

'How do you know I have a headache?'

He placed the mug on the bedside table and suppressed a grin.

'Why didn't you tell me you're not used to drinking wine, Marianne? I would have ordered you a soft drink. I apologise for my lack of foresight.'

'You don't have to sound so patronising,' Marianne snapped.

She took the coffee, sipped it gratefully and gave a great sigh.

'It is really I who should apologise, I suppose. I suspect that I said something 'way out of line, only I can't quite remember what it was.'

Nico continued to view her steadily.

'I can't say I noticed.'

'You didn't?'

Relief flooded through her.

'That's all right then.'

'No problem. I'll leave you to get dressed. We can discuss all the arrangements after breakfast, if that suits you.'

'What arrangements?'

His firm mouth turned up at the corners.

'You don't remember, do you?'

'Remember what?'

Nico experienced a strong desire to take her in his arms and kiss the bewilderment from her face. Instead, he went to the door and opened it.

'I'll see you at breakfast,' he said firmly, and closed it again.

Marianne lay in a warm, scented bath and tried to imagine what Nico had been talking about. A small feeling of unease gripped her insides. She dressed hurriedly in jeans and a pink cotton top and brushed the small knots from her hair, not bothering to tie it back, so that it lay in a shiny swathe about her shoulders. A dab of perfume and some lip gloss was all she needed in order to feel civilised once more before making her way somewhat gingerly to the kitchen.

'Good heavens, is that the time? It's almost twelve!' she exclaimed. 'What must you think of me? I usually wake up with the birds.'

'I know.'

His eyes swept over her body and

then lingered on the heavy veil of silk which framed her face. It was the most remarkable hair he had ever seen.

'I thought we'd have sausages and pancakes,' he informed her. 'We'll call it brunch instead of breakfast. Will that do? Pancakes are about all I can manage in the culinary department.'

Marianne gave a delighted smile.

'Pancakes are my favourite.'

'Good.'

They had almost finished their coffee when Nico observed in a casual voice, 'We'd better have our talk, now, Marianne.'

'Oh, all right. What about?'

Nico cleared his throat.

'Where would you like us to marry, and is it to be a civil or religious ceremony? I would prefer to be married in a church myself.'

Marianne choked.

'Married? But . . . I don't remember . . . did you ask me to marry you?'

Marianne strove vainly for some semblance of composure while her

121

thoughts tumbled about her head like clowns performing a bizarre circus act. There was the slightest hesitation before Nico answered quietly.

'In a manner of speaking, yes.'

'And did I agree?'

His face remained inscrutable.

'Yes.'

'Oh. You must forgive me, I'm a bit hazy about it. It must have been the wine.'

'No problem.'

He drained his mug and asked casually, 'You haven't changed your mind?'

'Oh, no. I shall be very pleased to marry you, Nico.'

'Thank you. So when is the wedding to be?'

Marianne took a deep breath. She'd done it! My goodness, she was a fast worker, although she said it herself. She'd made the man fall in love with her, and now he'd proposed. At the very thought her heart began to race. The fact that she couldn't quite remember the details was neither here nor there. The main thing was, she'd pulled it off!

It was what she'd been angling for all along, wasn't it? She'd come to Africa to hook Nicholas Logan, and hook him she had. Whoopee! So why did victory seem so wretchedly hollow?

She looked at Nico uncertainly.

'There's no hurry, is there?'

Deliberately, Nico put down his mug.

'I disagree. Once one decides to do something, there's no point in beating about the bush.'

'No, I suppose there isn't.'

'That's settled then. May I suggest the little church in Krugerville? I'll ring the vicar this morning.'

'This morning?'

He was gazing at her with that curious intentness again, almost as though he were trying to read her thoughts.

'I would like us to be married as soon as possible, Marianne. Say, in about two weeks' time.'

Marianne paled. Two weeks! Suddenly she wasn't so sure about anything any more.

Nico went on smoothly, 'Would that be long enough for you to find a wedding gown to your liking? Of course, we could always find a dressmaker, should you find our shops inadequate.'

Hastily Marianne pulled herself together.

'No. Yes . . . I mean . . . two weeks would be enough time.'

Enough time, she reflected, to visit Krugerville and find a travel agent so that she could book her air ticket back home to Scotland!

Nico, watching as the emotions flit over her expressive face, concealed his own feelings.

'Come with me, Marianne. I have something to give you.'

He took her by the hand and led her into the study where he removed a painting from one wall, opened a safe and extracted a small, velvet box.

'This ring has been passed down the generations in my family,' he told her, opening the box, to reveal an exquisite gold band set with rubies, sapphires and diamonds. 'I'd like you to have it, Marianne, unless, like my late wife, Carina, you consider it to be too old-fashioned, in which case I shall buy you something more to your taste.'

Marianne gazed at it.

'It's beautiful!'

She gave an unconscious sigh and looked up at him unhappily. It was a great pity she would only be wearing it for two weeks.

'Marianne?' His voice held a question. 'You wish to change your mind?'

'No, I shan't change my mind. Thank you for the ring, Nico.'

It was the first time she'd used his name. She gazed once more at the ring. It seemed to be the type of ring which symbolised a true, loyal and committed love between two people, and she had no right to be wearing it.

A small, unexpected tear escaped and

trickled down her cheek. Of all the most wretched situations to be in! What was happening to her? She ought to be doing a jig. Marianne mastered her tears and gave a small sniff, happily unaware of Nico's intent look.

'You're crying,' he said softly as he slipped the ring on to her finger. 'Are you a romantic, Marianne?'

'No. That is, I used to be before . . . ' She bit off the words, 'Before your brother let me down so callously.'

Controlling her emotions, Marianne continued firmly.

'I've become a sensible, realistic, level-headed person, with a no-nonsense approach to life and love.'

Nico, still watching her, smiled faintly.

'We'll see,' he murmured, and bent his head to kiss her with slow deliberation.

Marianne's breath locked in her lungs. Without thinking she slid her arms around Nico's neck and kissed him back because it was something she'd been wanting to do for days, and she wasn't regretting it one bit. It would be something to remember him by when she left Matonga. Marianne regained her breath together with her good sense. What was she thinking? This wasn't how she was supposed to be feeling at all!

Nico released her, his grey eyes smoky.

'Definitely a romantic,' he observed with masculine satisfaction, 'and passionate with it, which augers well for our future life together, does it not?'

Marianne had the grace to blush. She looked away hastily. All at once she knew exactly why she felt as she did. Despite all her good intentions she'd fallen headlong in love with Nicholas Logan! She gulped and took an urgent step backwards. What a fine mess she was making of everything!

'A small toast, I think,' Nico was saying.

He went to a cabinet in one corner of the room and poured two glasses of sherry. Marianne took her glass with a shaky hand and watched while Nico lifted his glass.

'To the lady with the beautiful hair. May she long continue to delight me.'

His next words left her speechless.

'I'm taking you into Krugerville this afternoon, Marianne, to collect my daughter, our daughter, that is.'

Marianne was compelled to gulp the rest of her drink. Things were moving altogether too fast for her!

She put her glass down and said carefully, 'You didn't tell me you were a father, Nico.'

'I didn't? How remiss of me. I have a six-year-old by the name of Jenna, who is at school in Krugerville and due to come home for half-term. At long last I can give her the mother she has been longing for. She'll be delighted to meet you.'

Marianne felt as though there was a rock in the pit of her stomach. He was marrying her in order to gain a mother for his daughter! It was a lowering thought, but she had no right to feel disappointed. Suddenly she felt sickened by the whole situation. If she had any courage whatsoever she would tell Nico the truth, ask his forgiveness and fly home immediately before any further harm was done. Wasn't her father always saying that two wrongs did not make a right?

When James had wronged her she should have done what her father had suggested. She should have considered herself well rid of the man and got on with her life, but by scheming to extract a petty revenge she had demeaned herself, even in her own eyes.

'Marianne? You've gone very pale. Would you like another drink?'

Marianne shook her head and fixed a bright smile on her face.

'I'm fine, Nico. You were saying?'

'After we have dropped Jenna you will be able to browse through the boutiques and wedding shops while I attend to some business. Jenna,' he repeated, 'will simply adore you.'

A remark not guaranteed to sooth Marianne's frayed emotions!

The drive home from Krugerville was a jolly one — at least, for Nico and his small daughter.

Jenna, delighted beyond measure to be going home to Matonga again, not to mention the prospect of a new mother, chattered non-stop.

'I'm glad you're so pretty,' she confided shyly to Marianne. 'You're far prettier than any of the other girls' mothers. What shall I call you, Marianne or Mummy?'

'Oh, Mummy, I think,' Nico intervened smoothly. 'After all, we'll be having other children who will all call her Mummy, too.'

Jenna clapped her small hands in delight.

'Oh, good. I'll help you to keep them in order.'

The car ate up the miles with a dignified purr while the wedding was discussed ad nauseam, so that eventually Marianne felt she would like the

130

luxury of a good scream. It was with relief that she saw the entrance to Matonga and suggested brightly that she would prepare the dinner while Jenna unpacked her small suitcase before taking her bath.

Two weeks, Marianne thought unhappily as she drifted off to sleep that night — two more weeks to be with Nico. She had better make the most of them, for she was quite certain that she would never, ever come to Africa again.

On Monday morning, they drove Jenna back to school with the promise that she would be allowed to become a day scholar the following term. The little girl beamed.

'Oh, thank you, Daddy! Will Mummy drive me to school every day?'

Nico glanced at Marianne.

'Probably. We haven't discussed it yet, darling.'

'Will you both come in with me now? I'll show you my dormitory, and I want to show Mummy off to my friends.'

'Why not?'

Marianne felt meaner than ever. How could she be so cruel? Jenna was going to be vastly disappointed when she realised that her new mummy was a fake, or rather, that there would be no new mummy at all. She stole a look at Nico's devastatingly handsome profile as he drove through the school gates. What about Jenna's father? Would he be disappointed, too? After all, he hadn't actually said that he loved her.

Marianne spent the next hour wandering around the town pretending to look for a wedding dress and feeling more and more wretched as the morning wore on. The boutiques were surprisingly sophisticated. There were several gowns she could have chosen, all much more to her taste than the wedding dress James had insisted upon, and which had long since been consigned to a charity shop in Inverness.

'Find anything?' Nico asked as he

ushered her into a coffee shop in the main street.

Marianne assumed her plastic smile.

'Oh, yes. There were one or two delightful gowns, and rows of satin shoes. I couldn't quite decide, so I'll leave it for a few days while I have a think about it.'

Nico reached into the pocket of his khaki bush jacket and extracted a cheque book.

'Which reminds me. I've made arrangements with my bank to deposit a quarterly allowance into your account.'

Marianne, feeling a little sick, took the cheque book. This was getting worse and worse. She opened the book, glanced at the figures and gasped.

'This is very generous of you, Nico.'

He inclined his head.

'My pleasure. As my wife, you will expect to be well provided for. Now, what will you have? A pot of tea and one of those delicious Danish pastries?'

It would be wonderful, Marianne thought as they drove back to Matonga, to really be married to Nico. He was unfailingly polite and had been nothing but considerate towards her. His small daughter was a poppet and she would like nothing better than to be the child's mother, live at Matonga and help Nico with his work.

She sighed deeply. What a confounded mess she'd got herself into!

When they reached Matonga, Nico suggested she might like to accompany him to the animal hospital to check on one or two animals.

'Remember that hartebeest calf? He's doing famously. We'll keep him a while longer and then begin a programme to release him back into the wild again.'

Marianne was genuinely pleased.

'Oh, how wonderful.'

Nico showed her around the small hospital. Marianne plied Nico with questions as they completed their tour of inspection.

At the end he said thoughtfully, 'When we're married you could work in the hospital, if you're interested, Marianne. We're frequently short staffed in here. The wardens prefer to work out in the reserve itself.'

Marianne's eyes lit up.

'That would be wonderful. I'd like that, Nico.'

Her pleasure evaporated as she remembered that she wouldn't be around to accept the offer.

At breakfast the following morning Nico informed Marianne that he had managed to find a replacement for Jemima.

'The wife of one of our African wardens would be prepared to work for a few hours each week. She will begin next Monday, and her name is Ntombela. I told her it would not be necessary to undertake any cooking, as the future Mrs Logan was more than competent.'

Marianne nodded, hiding her relief. At least when she had departed, Nico's housework and laundry would be taken care of. Before she left she would cook a batch of pies and casseroles and leave them in the freezer. That would tide him over for a few weeks. A great sadness engulfed her. If only things had not turned out this way! She resolved to drive into Krugerville at the end of the week and find the nearest travel agent. The sooner she could put all this behind her, the better.

Ironically, it was the same sentiment she had felt only a few short weeks ago when she'd left Scotland!

The week sped by, with Marianne growing more and more unhappy. Nico, on the other hand, appeared to be considerably relaxed. He hadn't attempted to kiss her again, which was just as well, Marianne thought. She would probably fling herself at that broad chest and weep all over his nice khaki bush jacket.

On Saturday morning Nico informed her that two of the wardens were ill with influenza, and he would have to assume some extra duties, one of which was to conduct a safari that evening.

He'd be sleeping at a hutted camp in the next valley in order to be on hand for the game drives, one at midnight and one at sun-up. Marianne's eyes lit up. She couldn't possibly go back to Scotland without taking part in such an experience.

'May I come along, too?' she begged. 'If there is enough room, that is.'

Nico shrugged.

'Why not? You'll enjoy it. I'll be leaving at five, so be ready. I suggest you have a bath before you go. The showers there are a little rudimentary, and you would be better off sleeping in your clothes. Take a sweater because it can get cool during the night, and remember to wear a pair of stout shoes, in case of snakes.'

'Where will I sleep?'

Nico paused.

'In my rondavel, of course.'

'I couldn't possibly. I'm not . . . I won't.'

'Relax, Marianne,' he drawled. 'There are twin beds.'

With that she had to be content. Anything to be able to experience a real safari!

It was dusk as they approached the camp, which consisted of a group of eight rondavels, or round huts, all with thatched roofs, built around a grassy area where a huge camp fire was already blazing, its smoke curling in great drifts towards the sky. To one side was a spacious communal meeting place filled with cane chairs bearing squashy cushions. The room had two open sides where screens of scarlet bougainvillaea, lemon-hued frangipani and snow-white jasmine grew. A row of tables stood along one wall, where the African cook would later place the food which had been prepared over the open fire.

Marianne's senses quickened as she climbed from the Jeep and inhaled a heady mixture of sweet-scented jasmine, barbecued meat, veld grass and scorched dust. It had been a hot day.

'We are quite safe within the enclosure,' Nico assured her, noting her faint look of apprehension as she stared out towards the open grassland beyond the fence. 'You may hear the odd elephant or lion during the night, but there is no need for concern. The worst that can happen is that a few inquisitive monkeys decide to venture over the fence.'

A number of guests were already seated around the campfire, chatting and enjoying the aperitifs which Abel, the cook, had dispensed with practised speed. Nico showed Marianne to their room and left her to tidy her hair, which had become loose from its knot during the ride from the house.

'Join me at the fire when you are ready,' he invited. 'As soon as all the guests have arrived I shall be giving a short talk, instructions, and so on, and then we will dine.'

'And after that?'

He smiled.

'Wait and see.'

Marianne examined the accommodation which, while fairly civilised, had a relaxed, outdoors feel to it. She grinned. There was even natural air conditioning! On a hot night one would welcome the breezes wafting in through the cracks, for the hut was built of stout logs where one could almost, but not quite, see through the chinks. And if one were brave enough in the face of all those monkeys, one could even leave the top half of the stable door open all night!

Marianne re-applied her lip gloss, dabbed more perfume behind her ears and let herself out of the hut. She was looking forward to the next few hours. They would have to sustain her over many a damp, grey Scottish evening once she had left South Africa, which reminded her — she really must make some excuse to drive into Krugerville on Monday, and book her ticket home.

Marianne approached the fire and looked around for Nico. His tall, tanned figure could be seen amongst a group of chattering tourists, and at the sight her heart gave a small jerk of pleasure. He was incredibly handsome. His dark head bent to listen politely to something one of the women was saying. She was an extraordinarily beautiful woman, with a huge smile turned full on, obviously for Nico's benefit. Long blonde hair cascaded over her shoulders and her large blue eyes gazed up at him adoringly.

At that moment, Nico lifted his head. His eyes locked with Marianne's but she was quite unable to interpret their expression. It would have amazed her had she known his thoughts.

'Ah, Marianne. May I introduce Miss Emma Hatton?' He added with a faint smile, 'Emma is a beauty queen, the current Miss England, in fact.'

He paused.

'And this,' he said indicating the man at Miss Hatton's side, 'is her companion. I believe he is already known to you.'

Nico watched Marianne intently from half-closed eyes before adding, 'My half-brother, James Logan.'

6

Marianne froze. From deep inside she summoned the will to look up into the face of the man who had let her down so badly only a matter of weeks previously. She felt nothing!

James's handsome, familiar face stirred not the slightest pang. It was as though he had already been relegated to the past. She greeted him in a disinterested voice.

'Oh, it's you. Hello, James.'

James Logan recovered his amazement. He had the grace to blush, his usual arrogant manner deserting him.

'W-well,' he stammered. 'I must say I'm surprised to find you here, Marianne. Not your usual style, is it?'

Marianne smiled sweetly.

'You wouldn't know my style if it hit you over the head, James.'

Tucking her hand into Nico's arm,

she continued clearly, 'What a good thing I decided to accompany my fiancé here this evening, or I'd have missed meeting you, and your . . . er, friend, Ms Hedding.'

'Hatton,' James snapped. 'Her name is Hatton. Did you say fiancé?'

'I'm a lucky man, am I not?' Nico intervened smoothly. 'Marianne has agreed to become my wife.'

James flushed an unbecoming red.

'You can't be serious!'

Nico eyed him coldly.

'I'm perfectly serious.'

'But . . . she's . . . we . . . ' James blustered.

There was a steely edge to Nico's tones.

'Yes?'

'Nothing,' James mumbled.

Nico turned away to speak to a middle-aged lady who wanted to ask a question about the transport. He had little time for his half-brother, the man who had had an affair with his wife, aided and abetted her departure from Matonga and then informed him callously of her demise in a car accident two weeks later. James, he knew from past experience, was a very persuasive young man, and thoroughly unscrupulous with it. Unfortunately, women fell for his not inconsiderable charm like ripe fruit from a tree, though why, he had no idea. He would need to make certain that Marianne did not fall under James's spell. It would be typical of the man to try to entice her away.

Nico raised his voice and asked the guests to assemble for a few minutes, when he welcomed them officially before issuing instructions concerning the game drives. Those guests who wished to view the game by night were asked to assemble at midnight, while those who preferred the dawn drive went early to their beds in order to prepare for the early start.

'I'm opting for the morning drive,' Miss Hatton told Marianne chattily. 'I need my beauty sleep. James will be taking hundreds more photographs of me in the morning as soon as the light is right. He's a stickler for perfection, you know.'

'Is he?' Marianne asked blandly, thinking of the many times she'd had to rearrange things in order to suit her demanding ex-fiancé.

'Oh, yes. James has asked me to marry him, but I'm not at all sure I want to live the rest of my life trying to live up to his exacting standards.'

The girl had more sense than Marianne would have credited her with.

'You're very wise,' she murmured politely.

Miss Hatton shrugged.

'As soon as he met me he ditched the girl he was engaged to.'

'Did he, indeed?'

'Oh, yes. She was a real bore, apparently. James says she couldn't hold a candle to me.'

She tossed her long blonde hair over one shoulder.

'But somehow a man who could do that to someone isn't really trustworthy, is he? I mean, how do I know he won't meet someone he fancies more than me, and leave me standing at the altar? I don't think I'll marry him at all.'

Dinner consisted of barbecued steak, spicy sausages, fire-baked potatoes and an astonishing variety of salad vegetables, followed by fresh fruit salad served in the scooped out halves of pineapples. Marianne finished the last delicious mouthful and put down her spoon.

'That was wonderful.'

Nico smiled at her indulgently.

'Yes, wasn't it? Is the safari living up to your expectations so far, Marianne?'

'Oh, definitely, but I'm longing for the next bit. I've decided to go on the midnight drive. Actually, I'd give anything to be able to view the animals at dawn, as well. Is there any chance of that?'

'Perhaps. I'll let you know later, once the others have made their choices.'

Just before midnight, a small group of guests assembled next to the large, open-sided vehicle as they had been instructed to do.

'Everyone ready?' Nico asked, informing them they could sit where they pleased. 'Providing everyone adheres to the rules, there should be no mishaps. In any event, I have my rifle with me.'

Marianne stood back politely to allow Nico's guests to climb aboard first. She was about to follow suit when James appeared out of the darkness. He grabbed her arm.

'You're a fast worker, aren't you, Marianne?' he taunted. 'Off with the old, on with the new! Only weeks ago you were going to marry me.'

'I can't think why,' Marianne replied sweetly. 'What a disastrous mistake it would have been, James. I'm glad I wised up in time. A man who can't be trusted to turn up on his wedding day isn't much of a catch, is he?'

'I would have phoned,' James said sulkily.

'I doubt it. You were too busy. Your career comes first, remember? You're a selfish man, James, and I'm not in the least sorry I won't be marrying you. Nico is twice the man you are.'

'Nico is a jerk,' James spat out. 'Always has been, always will be! He hasn't got what it takes to hold a woman. Look how easily he lost Carina to me. All I had to do was snap my fingers.'

Marianne had had enough of the conversation.

'Goodbye, James,' she said, and climbed into the truck.

There weren't many seats left by this time, and she had to content herself with one at the very rear. In front, on the bonnet of the vehicle in a specially constructed seat, a man was perched — Isaac, the African tracker. Marianne watched in fascination as he prepared to shine a searchlight into the darkness. How exciting it was going to be, viewing all the nocturnal species she had only ever seen in magazines. A cool, scented breeze fanned her cheeks as they drove along the track leading to one of the waterholes. The vast landscape around them looked awesome in the moonlight and a little scary.

Nico pointed out a lone giraffe silhouetted against the skyline, and as Marianne looked out over the darkened veld a small thrill of excitement gripped her as she listened to the unfamiliar night noises — the rustle of grass, the faint cry of an owl, the distant bark of a baboon. It was refreshing to be driving through this remote corner of the earth at midnight. What's more, she had made the discovery that the heart she'd thought was broken was in fact completely intact, pulsing with life and love. Even more curious was the fact that she had no further desire for revenge.

James was a man to be pitied. He was far too self-centred a person to ever be happy in himself. He was a taker, and she needed a giver. Yes, her heart was pulsing with love — for Nicholas Logan and his beautiful land.

At last she felt able to face the fact that her love for him could not be denied. He was the only man she wanted, and always would. So why cut off her nose to spite her face? She would telephone her parents at the earliest opportunity and tell them that she had, after all, found a man she could trust. Having made up her mind, Marianne felt a surge of pure happiness.

She would go through with their marriage after all, and do her best to make it a success. She was under no illusions about Nico's reasons for marrying her, but somehow it didn't seem to matter. He hadn't actually said that he loved her, but she had enough love for the two of them, and given time, patience and a determined effort, she would make him love her!

She was jolted out of her thoughts by the woman in the next seat, who gave a restrained shriek and pointed a shaking finger into the night.

'Look!'

Obediently Marianne looked down

the beam of light and there, walking towards the Jeep with loose-limbed, feline grace, was a leopard. Nico stopped the vehicle while Isaac put a finger on his lips to warn them all to keep quiet, but there was no need. Everyone was riveted to their seats with either excitement or fear. Marianne watched the leopard slink towards them and shivered. Seeing such an animal on a TV screen where it looked quite cuddly was very different from reality. This animal was both powerful and deadly, and fast.

She glanced at Nico in faint alarm, but he had left his rifle lying beside him on the seat. If the leopard had decided to attack, it would have been on them before they could have moved, but Nico seemed to know that this would not be the case. The leopard brushed against the side of the vehicle where Marianne sat. It was so close, she could smell it. She could almost have put out a hand and touched it, too — an exhilarating experience, and to think there would be many more like this now that she had decided to make Matonga her home!

At the waterhole they watched a group of elephants come trundling up to drink and cavort, spraying themselves with water from their trunks. There were one or two antelope and some zebra, too, and a large hippopotamus, which grunted every time his head appeared above the surface of the water.

After an hour of driving and viewing a number of animals going about their usual nightly business, Nico turned the vehicle towards the camp.

'Enjoy it?' he asked Marianne when the last of the group had departed to their huts.

'Oh, it was quite wonderful!'

She turned an enraptured face towards his, so that Nico, quite unable to restrain himself, took her in his arms and kissed her fiercely. The force of his feelings stunned him. He had entered the engagement sincerely but as a convenience, with his heart intact. But somewhere between the campfire and the waterhole this evening he'd lost it, to this dark-haired woman who had become irresistible to him. He appeared to have fallen hard!

He wanted her for his wife more than he'd ever wanted anything in his life, but now was not the time to tell her so. Despite her willingness to be hurried into marriage, he was unclear about her real motives. He sensed her natural reserve, but was a patient man. Given time, she would fall in love with him. He would marry her and then woo her.

'May I join you?' James's voice asked silkily from behind Marianne's shoulder.

Nico lifted his head and stared at the other man with distaste. Had the fellow no manners?

'What do you want, James?'

'There is something you need to know and something I need to say.'

'Say it, then,' Nico clipped.

James gave a low, mocking laugh.

'You're a prime fool, Nicholas. You

can't see what's going on under your own nose. I wish to point out that Marianne, here, is not quite what she seems. I don't know what she's playing at, but the fact is, she is still my fiancée. We were about to be married when I was called away on this assignment.'

He glanced from one to the other with malicious satisfaction.

'That's all I wanted to say.'

Nico went very still.

'Is that the truth, Marianne?' he demanded in a voice devoid of expression.

Marianne frowned.

'Well, yes, it is, but let me explain . . .'

Nico's expression was all at once remote. Only his eyes betrayed his cold rage.

'No need,' he clipped in a hard, bitter voice. 'I have enough imagination to know just exactly what the true situation is.'

James grinned.

'I'll see you back in England,

Marianne, my love, once I've finished up here with Emma's photographic shoot.'

He sauntered off, whistling.

'Nico,' Marianne began urgently, laying a hand on his arm, 'let me explain. It's not quite like that. You see, James . . .'

' . . . is a first rate jerk,' Nico grated. 'You have no need to defend the man, Marianne. I know what he's like.'

He shook her hand off his arm.

'I have no idea what makes you and my obnoxious brother tick, but I suspect the two of you get your kicks out of wrecking other people's lives and happiness.'

Marianne gasped.

'That's not true! Please listen.'

'No. You will leave my house by lunchtime tomorrow, Miss Chattan, when I will personally escort you off the premises. You can go to Sunrise Lodge to be with your lover, and good riddance to the two of you. I never wish to set eyes on either of you again.'

Ignoring Marianne's pained cry, Nico strode away without looking back. Marianne stumbled back to the rondavel in an unhappy daze. How could it be that twice in as many months her dreams were in pieces?

Nico's words had been chillingly final and he hadn't even given her an opportunity to explain herself. She sat on the bed and tried to reason with herself. In the morning she would try to explain things again. Everything usually seemed brighter once the sun was up.

Still fully clothed, Marianne lay on top of her single bed and turned her face to the wall. She pretended to be asleep when she heard Nico come in much later and fling himself on to his bed. Once his breathing had evened she relaxed a little, but found it difficult to sleep. In consequence she spent a long, restless night wondering if she would be given the opportunity to straighten things out.

When she awoke, the sun was blazing in through the window. Nico was nowhere to be seen. Marianne sat up in dismay. He hadn't even woken her in time for the dawn drive! With a heavy heart she washed her face, applied fresh make-up, straightened the beds and let herself out of the hut.

Breakfast was already underway. Embarrassed at being so late, she joined the other tourists. Miserably aware of Nico's cold silence and James's knowing smirks, she crumbled her slice of toast on to her plate and made a futile effort to eat it. After gulping a few mouthfuls of coffee she went to stand quietly beside Nico's Jeep as she waited for him to hand over to one of the wardens.

Without a word, he motioned Marianne into the front seat and shut the passenger door.

'Nico,' she began, once they had left the camp and were driving up the hill, 'about last night. I believe you have the incorrect impression.'

'Shelve it, Marianne,' he interrupted in a voice as cold and hard as steel.

'The subject is closed.'

At the house Marianne jumped out, shaking with rage, so that shutting the Jeep door was difficult. She managed it and strode through the garage into the kitchen, taking large gulps of air in order to steady herself. She had never felt so angry and miserable in all her life, not even when James had betrayed her. Nico was the most awesome, infuriating, pig-headed male she had ever had the misfortune to meet — and she loved him!

'Kindly be ready at twelve,' he told her expressionlessly.

Marianne pulled the ring from her finger and flung it down on to the kitchen table.

'I'll be ready in ten minutes,' she said furiously.

'Fine.'

Nico pocketed the ring and strode off down the passage, whistling between his teeth. Marianne then went to her room and flung her clothes into her suitcase, ran a brush through her hair and went to find him.

'I'm ready,' she informed him in a cold voice.

How she kept the tears from falling, she would never know. Without a word Nico picked up her luggage and preceded her to the garage where he stowed it in the trunk of her hired car. Still coldly polite, he opened the door and stood aside.

Marianne did not bother to thank him. She grabbed the handle, slammed it shut and wound down the window.

'Goodbye, Nico,' she said in a voice which wobbled only slightly. 'If you'd bothered to verify the true facts about me and James, you and I might have had a good life together because despite my previous good intentions and the voices of my commonsense, I've had the misfortune to fall deeply in love with you. You probably won't believe me when I say how sorry I am.'

She broke off with a huge sniff.

Nico's eyes widened.

'Marianne . . . '

Marianne waved a dismissive hand.

'No, I won't listen to anything further you may have to say.'

Furiously she fired the engine and slipped the gear into reverse.

'Since you were happy to assume the worst about me, it shows me that you are no better than your stinking brother. I wish I'd never set eyes on either of you!'

She stamped on the accelerator and reversed down the drive. The sooner she put this place behind her, the better!

7

Marianne did not bother to go to Sunrise Lodge after all. She turned the car in the opposite direction and drove straight to Johannesburg International Airport, arriving just in time to hand back the hired car and obtain a ticket on a South African Airways flight to Heathrow.

From Kings Cross she took the train to Inverness and then caught the village bus to Inchfarrel, arriving in the late afternoon. The village had never looked so pretty, with early snow mantling the hills behind the house and frosting the dark fringe of pines covering its lower slopes.

Marianne hauled her suitcase up the front steps of the house, rang the bell since she had no key with her, and summoned a bright smile. Mrs Chattan, busy in the kitchen, wiped floury hands on her apron and went to open the door.

'Darling!' she cried. 'We had no idea you were arriving today. Why did you not warn us?'

'Hello, Mother.' Marianne kissed her cheek. 'Where's father?'

'At the surgery, dear. Come inside, I'll put the kettle on.'

Mrs Chattan bustled back to the kitchen while Marianne carried her luggage upstairs to the bedroom. She looked around the pretty, familiar room with its white furniture, pink floral curtains and matching bedspread, and all she saw was the rondavel with the grass roof and the gaps between the logs. She sat down on the bed and sighed. What now?

She supposed she would make a life for herself and go through all the motions of living but the fact remained that she would never, ever forget Nicholas Logan or the Matonga Reserve. They were both in her blood now.

Sternly she roused herself. She despised self pity and it would not do to sit and mope. The sooner she put the whole episode from her mind and picked up the severed threads of her life, the better. Tomorrow she would telephone Mr Longmore and ask for her old job back again.

Marianne slipped into her old routine without difficulty.

She offered to work four extra shifts at the animal clinic, joined the flower club in her spare time, went Christmas shopping with her mother and spent every moment being as busy as possible. It helped to deaden the pain.

One Saturday she even took herself into Dingwall and bought some wool and a pattern, which caused her mother's eyebrows to rise rather sharply. As a rule the dear child hated knitting!

'Marianne,' Mrs Chattan said carefully one evening as they sat in the living-room and waited for the doctor to come in, 'is there something worrying you, dear? You've not been quite yourself since you returned from your South African holiday. You've never said, but did you meet a man, perhaps?'

As usual, her mother's insight was painfully accurate.

'Yes, Mother, as a matter of fact, I did.'

'Do you care to tell me about it?'

So Marianne did. She left nothing out, and ended with a tearful, 'So you see, Mother, there's no future in a relationship with a Logan, is there? Oh, Mother, I'm so miserable.'

'Yes, dear. I was, too.'

Marianne stared.

'What did you say?'

'I said, I was miserable for a while, too. You see, before I agreed to marry your father, I thought I was in love with his cousin, Hamish Chattan.'

'Uncle Hamish? Mother, I never knew that.'

'No, dear.'

'What happened?'

'Oh, Hamish threw me over for someone else he met. So you see, I understand how you feel, dear. I was most unhappy when I discovered that it was your father I really loved, because by this time he had come mistakenly to believe that it was I who was feckless, and he wouldn't give me the time of day.'

Marianne's eyes widened in amazement.

'Good heavens, Mother. I thought the people of your generation were quite without faults and failings.'

Mrs Chattan laughed gently.

'Not at all. We made our share of mistakes. Your father was particularly blind and stubborn.'

'What did you do, then, to change his mind?'

Mrs Chattan gave her daughter a thoughtful look.

'Do you really wish to know, dear?'

'Yes, Mother.'

'And you truly love this man?'

'Yes. I've discovered that I'm totally

miserable without him. I'd give anything to start all over again, Mother. I love the wild, harsh landscape there, too. It's like nothing else I've ever experienced.'

She went on to describe the delights of Matonga at some length, while her mother listened patiently and gave an inward sigh.

'I can see that I shall have to part with my secrets.' She smiled. 'We can't have you pining away, can we? If this Nicholas Logan is as fine a man as your father is, Marianne, you must fight for him. You must go back to Africa. You must not run away from the situation.'

'How can I? He told me to leave, and he doesn't love me.'

Marianne sighed.

'Pooh,' Mrs Chattan said confidently.

She was a woman who was adept at reading between the lines. From what she could divine, Dr Logan was every bit as smitten with her daughter as Marianne herself was with him.

'Now listen to me, dear. You will have

to plan a battle strategy. Does the man have any weaknesses?'

'Well, he likes a nice pudding for dessert.'

Mrs Chattan smiled in triumph.

'Perfect. I have a marvellous book of recipes.'

★   ★   ★

It was a long, hot, December day in the southern hemisphere and the sun was once more beating mercilessly down upon the African veld.

Nico nosed his car through the gates of Matonga and turned on to the road to Krugerville where he intended to collect his small daughter to take home for the long summer holiday. He had been forced to take leave for the next three weeks, having been unable to find a babysitter for Jenna, and despite his love for her, the prospect of having to spend endless days in the company of a small child was not altogether appealing. Besides, the Christmas spirit

appeared to have eluded him altogether.

'May we have a Christmas tree,
Daddy?' Jenna asked that evening.

Nico stirred the pot of stew which
was bubbling on the cooker. The
darned stuff was too watery. How the
heck did one thicken it?

'Sure. We'll find one tomorrow,
Jenna.'

'But where will we find one? There
aren't any fir trees at Matonga.'

He cast his daughter an exasperated
glance.

'That's true. I guess we'll have to
take a drive into Krugerville to buy
one.'

'Can we buy some decorations as
well?'

'Sure.'

'With silver balls and green-striped
sugar sticks and small red Santas with
toys in their sacks?'

'Sure,' Nico agreed vaguely.

How the heck did one get a jelly to
set? Jenna particularly liked jelly, and

he'd followed the instructions on the packet with meticulous care, but the result appeared to be fit only for the garbage can.

'You're the best daddy in the world,' Jenna said happily.

Nico burned his fingers on the hotplate and cursed under his breath.

'Thanks, angel. Would you care to set the table?'

Jenna went to the dresser to find the knives and forks.

'OK, Daddy, but I wish Marianne were here. Your cooking's not a patch on hers, you know.'

Nico almost dropped the pan.

'Don't you wish Marianne would come back, Daddy?' Jenna persisted.

'Er . . . sure.'

If only the child knew! He hadn't been able to sleep for nights.

'Why did she go away then? I thought she was going to take me to buy my bridesmaid dress, but you said she had to go home to see her mother. When is she coming back, Daddy?'

Nico sighed heavily.

'Can we discuss this another time? Dinner's ready, and after dinner we'll play that game of snap.'

Jenna, suitably diverted, agreed.

Once Jenna was in bed, Nico cleaned up the kitchen and took his mug of coffee out on to the darkened patio. Marianne used to sit out here and watch the birds.

He drained his mug and sat listening to the sounds of the African night. The laugh of a hyena and the sound of a lion roaring in the distance for once gave him no pleasure. He thought idly that if Marianne were there, how different things would be. They'd savour the quiet dark together and then he'd kiss her, and then they'd go inside.

He remembered that last safari, and smiled mirthlessly. She had been so delightful in her enthusiasm, and then he'd spoiled it all by allowing James's spiteful comments to mislead him. The fact that he'd regretted it almost as soon as her car had disappeared was no comfort. He'd driven to Sunrise Lodge the following day and demanded the truth from his sulky brother, but it had been too late. Marianne hadn't even checked in. She'd flown home to Scotland.

He thought of the manner in which he'd forced a reluctant James to give him her address, and was faintly ashamed. He was confident that his half brother would be keeping out of his way for some time to come.

Nico rinsed his mug at the kitchen sink and went into his study to read the latest veterinary journal, which had arrived in the morning post. He removed the wrapping and opened the title page but found himself unable to concentrate. In frustration he tossed it aside and sat thinking of Marianne. Those desserts she'd made him had been out of this world.

Nico looked into the future and was appalled by what he saw — long, lonely evenings like this one, without the woman he loved The thought was intolerable.

Once Christmas was over he would drive to Johannesburg, leave Jenna with his sister and her husband, and book a flight to Scotland. He would find Marianne, apologise for his insensitivity and persuade her to marry him. This time they would both be totally honest with each other, and he'd tell her something of which he knew she was completely unaware — the fact that he'd fallen in love with her the first time he'd seen her!

In the morning, Nico bought his daughter the biggest tree he could find, complete with every Christmas decoration which took her fancy. They drove home to Matonga and spent a happy afternoon making the house look so festive that Jenna went to bed that evening with shining eyes.

Ntombela, the wife of one of the wardens, arrived at nine o'clock the following morning in order to clean the house as usual. Nico, taking advantage of her presence, left Jenna in her charge and drove into Krugerville to buy his daughter a Christmas present, promising to be home by four o'clock, when Ntombela's husband would arrive to fetch her.

Jenna occupied herself with her dolls, ate her snack obediently and then sat with her crayons at the kitchen table, making Christmas cards. By four o'clock when Ntombela was ready to leave, Nico was nowhere to be seen.

'Don't worry, I can look after myself until my daddy comes home,' Jenna assured the woman. 'You can go home now if you like.'

'All right,' Ntombela agreed without reluctance.

Alone in the silent house, Jenna went from room to room and became nervous. She began to cry, curled in a small ball upon the sofa. She was sobbing so hard that she failed to hear the arrival of the small vehicle which drove down the drive and parked itself out of sight behind the garage.

Purposefully, Marianne climbed from the red Mini she'd hired and hefted out her two suitcases. Those recipe books were heavier than she'd realised. She lugged the cases up the stairs into the kitchen and looked about with an assessing eye. The house appeared to be tidy enough, but someone had neglected to water the African violets on the window sill.

She went down the passage and paused at the living-room door where Jenna, her small face streaked with tears, had just fallen asleep. Marianne woke her gently.

'Hello, Jenna, I'm back.'

Jenna's grey eyes widened in dazed delight.

'Mummy! You've come back.'

'Of course, I have. Where's your father?'

'He went to Krugerville to buy things and he hasn't come home yet. Ntombela was watching me, but she had to go home, and then I became frightened.'

'I see. Well, I'm here now, love, and I've an idea up my sleeve. Shall we get you bathed and then you can help me with the dinner?'

An hour later, Nico's car raced down the drive and squealed to a halt. He climbed out wearily and ran a hand through his hair. Hopefully Ntombela would have had the sense to wait with Jenna. How was he to know the fan belt would give trouble and he'd have to return to Krugerville to have it fixed?

He climbed up the steps into the kitchen and halted in amazement. A delicious aroma was coming from the oven, the table had been set with the best cutlery and a spectacular dessert was resting on the worktop, complete with whipped cream, nuts and glacé cherries.

Good grief! Ntombela had really excelled herself today! He'd pay her extra for her time. Humming, he went down the passage and hid Jenna's presents behind his desk before going to find her.

'Jenna,' he yelled.

'In the living-room, Daddy. We're

looking at pictures of bridesmaid dresses.'

Nico sighed. Jenna was still harping on about weddings Then he stopped in the doorway and stared, his face pale beneath his tan as his heart rate went into overdrive.

'Marianne?'

'Oh, it's you,' Marianne said casually.

She straightened the page so that Jenna might view it more clearly.

'What took you so long? I thought you were supposed to be home by four.'

Nico regained his power of speech.

'I . . . um, had car trouble. What are you doing here?'

Marianne feigned astonishment.

'I thought that would have been obvious.'

'Jenna,' Nico suggested, not taking his eyes from Marianne's face, 'I'd like some time alone with Marianne. Will you go and tidy your bedroom?'

'OK, Daddy.'

Jenna rose obediently, kissed them both and observed dreamily as she departed, 'Rose pink, I think. I prefer it to the turquoise.'

Carefully Nico closed the living-room door.

'I think you owe me an explanation.'

His steely eyes turned smoky.

'There's a fabulous dinner waiting in the kitchen, Jenna is in a state of ecstasy and I find you sitting in my living-room, ticking me off for being late as though you were my wife.'

'Well, I will be soon, won't I?' Marianne pointed out calmly.

'I don't understand. I expressly remember asking you to leave my home. What are you playing at, Marianne?'

Carefully, Marianne moistened her lips with her tongue. It was now or never.

'I'm not playing at anything. I'm deadly serious.'

She rose, walked up to him and placed her arms about his neck.

'I think actions are better than words, don't you? You are the only man for me,

Nicholas Logan, and I am going to show you rather than say it. I am going to kiss you senseless.' And she did!

When Nico had recovered himself, he asked gruffly, 'To what do I owe this immensely satisfying display of affection?'

'Oh,' Marianne said airily, 'my mother told me to.'

Nico gaped.

'Your mother!'

'Yes. She's a fount of wisdom. She said that I must be prepared to fight for the man I want, even if he doesn't love me, so I have come armed with kisses and books and books of dessert recipes and I'll do my best to — '

She got no further, for Nico caught her to his chest and kissed her in the manner of a man deeply in love.

'Who said anything about desserts? I'd far rather have you, my darling. I love you to distraction, so we'll have no more talk of not loving.'

'Oh, do you? That's all right, then. I'd better phone Mother and tell her to

178

buy the air tickets, and she can go ahead and buy that pale blue wedding hat she's longing for.'

'As soon as possible, my love.'

After a few minutes Jenna peeped around the door.

'I'd like a baby brother if it can be arranged,' she announced, adding plaintively, 'I'm hungry. Can we have our dinner now? Mummy says the dessert will make you fall in love with her, Daddy.'

Reluctantly Nico lifted his mouth from Marianne's.

'Yes, angel, it can be arranged, but all these things take a little time to practice. And as for the dessert, I don't need one when I have your mother.'

DIVIDED LOYALTIES

Phyllis Demaine

When Heather's fiancé, Adrian, is offered a wonderful job in America their future seems rosy. However, Adrian's brother, Carl, a widower, asks for Heather's help with his small, deaf son. Help which, as a speech therapist, Heather is qualified to give. But things become complicated when Carl goes abroad on business and returns with Gisel, to whom his son takes an instant dislike. This puts Heather in the position of having to choose between the boy's happiness and her own.

ZABILLET OF THE SNOW

Catherine Darby

For Zabillet, a young peasant girl growing up in the tiny French village of Fromage in the mid-fourteenth century, a respectable marriage is the height of her parents' ambitions for her. But life is changing. Zabillet's love for a handsome shepherd is tested when she is invited to join the La Neige household, where her mistress, Lady Petronella, has plans for her grandson, Benet. And over all broods the horror of the Great Death that claims all whom it touches.

PERILOUS JOURNEY

Caroline Joyce

After the execution of Charles I, Louisa's Royalist father considers it too dangerous for her to stay in England and arranges for her to go to the Isle of Man with Armand de la Tremouille, the nephew of the island's Royalist Governor. Their ship is boarded by Parliamentarians who plan to sail for Ireland, but a storm causes them to be ship-wrecked on the Calf of Man. Magnus Stapleton, the Parliamentarian chief, becomes infatuated with Louisa, but she has fallen in love with Armand.

THE GYPSY'S RETURN

Sara Judge

After the death of her cruel father, Amy Keene's stepbrother and stepsister treated her just as badly. Amy had two friends, old Dr. Hilland and the washerwoman, Rosalind, with her fatherless child Becky. When Rosalind falls ill, Amy is entrusted with a letter to be given to Becky on her marriage. When the letter's contents are discovered, it causes Amy both mental and physical suffering and sets the seal of fate upon Rosalind's gypsy friend, Elias Jones.

WEB OF DECEIT

Margaret McDonagh

A good-looking man turned up on Louise's doorstep one day, introducing himself as Daniel Kinsella, an Australian friend of her brother-in-law, Greg. He said he had come to stay whilst he did some research — apparently Greg had written to her about it. Louise's initial reaction was to turn him away, but he was very persuasive. However, she was to discover that Daniel had bluffed his way into her life, and soon she found herself caught up in his dangerous mission.